ON ANOTHER PLANE

A Collection of Science Fiction and Fantasy Short Stories

ON ANOTHER PLANE

A Collection of Science Fiction
and Fantasy Short Stories

ISBN 978-0-9549287-2-8

Published by AudioArcadia.com 2015

CONTENTS

DAVID DEACON came to short story writing later in life. He considers the strongest influence on his work to be the fifteen years during which, every so often, he prepared and conducted secular naming, marriage and funeral ceremonies.

Music figures in much of David's writing. His first published stories appeared in "Blue Light", the journal of the Duke Ellington Society UK.

TOMORROW IN METROPOLIS

Reference 48804/529-037-9 preferred to think of herself as 'Niney', a pet name derived from her final digit.

She was taking a break from inserting simulated tulips in her allocated square of the roof garden. Her hip, her third, was fizzing and the small of her original back was aching.

She had remembered that she should bend her knees and crouch rather than lean over from a standing position, but she resisted the instructions.

At least the twinges were hers, hers alone; and she was jiggered if anyone was going to tell her what to do, especially not some patronising hologram installed by the authorities, however regularly it was up-dated.

Niney ignored the prurience of the heli-pilots hovering around her and took pleasure in lying back, elbows on the astroturf, her knees up and apart to enjoy the breeze that played around her private replacement parts. She knew it shocked and entertained Two-Two, her companion, Reference 51007, et cetera, 502-2.

'Goodness knows,' Niney declared airily, signalling that she was about to say something she knew Two-Two would find delightfully outrageous, 'they charge more than enough for my air inhalation ration.'

Niney looked up at Two-Two seated on her heli-zimmer, laughed raucously and indulged in three expensive deep breaths. Two-Two looked around them, worried that a Community Monitor might be within earshot.

'Two-Two, my sweet, I shall miss you, if…, when…' She sighed.

'Look, we're the last of the old school, aren't we? Surely we can do something about your summons.'

Two-Two shrugged, turned down her mouth and slowly moved her head from side to side. Her voice box, her second, was worn out.

Niney continued, 'They'll be after me as well soon, the buggers. Have to make the best of it while I can. Seize the day, eh? Live, breathe and be merry, for tomorrow we... we take their Journey of a Lifetime.' She grimaced. 'Oh, Two-Two, there must be some way out. For me, for you.'

Her mind felt its way to the last decamonth and the untimely loss of her designated post-meno paramour, sweet, witless Sixie, 036. The bereavement acceleration drops and memory eraser had helped her get through much of her loss; but the scent of his maleness lingered still.

They had summoned him for his JOLI, his Journey of a Lifetime Itinerary, earlier than his estimated time of departure. For soon after Wintafest®, he had exceeded his methane release quota. There were rumours that the introduction of methane meters was a ploy to reduce numbers by the Population Unit, now popularly known as PU.

Niney did not intend to follow Sixie or Two-Two just yet. She had recently gained a little respite. Her MO, male offspring 230, or 'Noughtie' as she called him, was a NAG, Neighbourhood Assessment Grass, and he had shown her the latest index.

Both The Southern Confederacy and Bangladesh were now completely submerged and, consequently, her own estimated time of departure was adjusted proportionately. Her summons was deferred, but loomed nevertheless. If Niney were to insert her simulated rose blooms again, she would need to resist, drawing on what Noughtie referred to as her 'cussedness'.

It always annoyed Reference 488, et cetera, 230 that his OH, Ovarian Host, insisted on calling him Noughtie well into his adulthood. Today, she was being more cussed than usual. It was typical of her to blame him. He felt guilt rising again in his stomach and was in danger of losing his hold on his sense of civic duty.

He said again, more loudly, 'You know as well as I do, there is nothing we can do, OH. We have to obey the law.'

It surprised him that his OH and he had managed to reach the platform. So far, her resistance had been manageable. Somehow, he had succeeded in cajoling her on to the monorail and staying on as far as the Necrocity interchange.

To his greater surprise, he had indeed enticed her on to the one-way descalator, he trying to talk softly, she yelling, as they travelled. The heated exchange was testing for him, dragging from his very guts acquiescence to maternal authority.

The Journey of a Lifetime hologram counsellor had briefed him well. He exhibited all the tolerance and empathy he could muster, keeping eye contact, acknowledging her anxieties and offering inducements. The doc-who bag had cost him an inconvenient number of asias, but his strategy seemed to be working as his ovarian host accepted each proffered inducement, fine coat, matching hat, scarf and gloves.

He festooned her with jewellery, filling her arms with flowers (two of them authentic) and chocolates (ten per cent cocoa). 230 was relieved they had arrived at the allocated departure point without the unpleasantness of calling in Journey of a Lifetime Enforcement Officers.

The transporter was already at the platform, doors open. The most tasteful of interiors glowed softly before them. Beside a simulated rosewood table elegantly laid for afternoon tea, the hologram of a young man appeared, smartly suited in Niney's favourite shade of blue. He smiled, holding out his hand. 'It's time, Niney. Welcome aboard for your Journey of a Lifetime.' His accent was impeccable, his voice smoky, inviting yet firm.

The theme from Rachmaninov's second piano concerto began to play. 230 was pleased he had remembered that her favourite vidzip was *Brief Encounter* from the first half of the twentieth century.

Following his counsellor's advice for this tricky moment, 230 chipped in, 'They tell me it's a great journey.'

His ovarian host made the fierce face which stirred his innards. She was pursing her lips and moving her eyes rapidly from side to side. She was what 033, his sperm progenitor, used to call 'impossible'.

The small crowd at the neighbouring carriage was waving and calling, 'Bye, Gramps!' They, at least, were behaving normally; his OH, however, was becoming an embarrassment.

He repeated the counsellor's mantra to himself, 'Be patient. It will soon be over'.

Niney was looking down at her feet. He followed her gaze: all he could see were the new shoes he had bought her.

'Oh, look!' she exclaimed. Her tone signalled that something was severely wrong.

Whatever it was, he must see to it immediately. If he did not, the consequences could be even severer. On the other hand, should it be 'more severe'?

She had him doubting his judgement again. He automatically placed his hand over his mouth and cleared his throat. He squinted. Then he corrected himself. It didn't look nice to squint. It made him look stupid, she told him.

He leaned forward. He could see nothing irregular.

'Oh, Noughtie, look!'

He bent over to peer at her shoes. It happened so painfully and suddenly that he was caught off guard. It began with a jarring, extremely hard blow, squarely to his jawbone.

Niney heard a hard crack. It was probably his chin rather than her knee, she decided, for her gardening kneepad was made of hard material. His head flew up, his arms splayed and his back arched.

She moved in, pushing her knee between his legs and then up hard against his groin. The blow had to be upward to crush the testicles against the pubic symphysis. She had learned the manoeuvre in the U3A Militia.

She heard a gratifying 'Aargh!' from him and looked around for Two-Two. As planned, Niney's loyal friend was speeding on her heli-zimmer from the direction of her own carriage.

Niney's adversary doubled over. She daintily sidestepped to his rear, placed her hands firmly on each side of his hips and swivelled him around towards the carriage.

Two-Two accelerated and swung her heli-zimmer against his buttocks. He lurched forward, staggering between the carriage doors. With his head down, he plunged headfirst through the hologram, collided with the mock Charles III on the far side, and collapsed.

Two-Two made a thumbs-up sign to her friend, but Niney was attending to the work in hand, overseeing Noughtie's demise. Two-Two mouthed 'Good-bye', waited a moment, negotiated a careful three-point turn and returned dutifully to the door of her own allotted carriage. She turned her head for the last time to look at her friend, mouthed 'Good luck', paused, raised her right hand in farewell, held it still a while, then entered her carriage, taking care not to knock the paintwork.

Noughtie was in an untidy crumpled heap. Niney pressed the one red button before her. There was a hiss and the two doors slid swiftly to meet at the centre, breaking the seal on the Zyklon-B gas pellet. She could see he was recovering from his fall.

He raised himself to a kneeling position, found his feet and turned to face the doors and her, clutching his groin, grimacing and gasping. That would be the gas, she surmised, as well as the dual impact of pain and surprise. Noughtie's expression looked ugly - and a touch comical.

Through the haze and beyond, through the sealed windows, 230 saw his ovarian host rubbing her right knee, biting her bottom lip. The awful music was growing louder. He staggered to the doors.

Niney saw her male offspring banging his fists in dumb show, the flesh whitening where it struck the soundproofed reinforced window. She recognized the look of pain, bewilderment and anger: when he was three, a neighbour's female offspring had pulled his hair and, weed that he was, instead of retaliating, he had stood still, feet apart, howled and wet himself.

He was mouthing something. Perhaps it was, 'OH, open this coupling door.' She could not be sure. In extreme circumstances, he could resort to the most awful language. Niney thought the 'c' word demonstrated a paucity of vocabulary. Noughtie had never been much of a reader.

He was sinking to his knees. His trousers would get dusty down there. He was wearing his best suit, too. Mind you, he had not chosen the right footwear to go with it, nor for the occasion, come to that. You would think that awful ovarian receptor of his could have advised him better. Some people had no taste. Moreover, look, he had no sense of decorum.

The other carriage doors hissed in unison. The transporter moved towards the tunnel. A young offspring from the neighbouring party waved and ran beside the next carriage, another was skipping between Niney and her own offspring.

'Goodbye, goodbye! Happy deathday!' they called.

There would be a scene with that awful female. Their offspring would make a fuss. Nevertheless, Niney would feign distress and describe how her devoted Noughtie had offered to take her place, how it all happened so fast and how, before she could do anything, there he was, waving, smiling dutifully at her.

Whatever they said, she knew she was safe, for the time being. If she had to, she could invoke the double jeopardy rule.

Niney picked up her bouquet and chocolates, clasped the collar of her new coat with her freshly ringed hand, the bangles on her new bracelet jangling, and turned towards the exit.

It would be crowded at pedestrian level.

She wanted to get home before the simulated April showers due at 1800 hours.

IAN C DOUGLAS. After a nerdy childhood spent in the company of Tolkien, Lovecraft, and a certain Time Lord, Ian C Douglas ran away to see the World. This quest for adventure landed him in countless scrapes, before finding himself teaching in East Asia.

After ten years, he returned to his native England, and graduated with an MA Distinction in Creative Writing. Since then he has written everything from computer games to children's apps. Several of his stories have won prizes and some of his writing has appeared at the V&A's Toy Museum.

Science Fiction has always been Ian's first love. He is currently writing his third book in the Zeke Hailey series, a collection of SF novels for young adults set on Mars.

Ian lives near Sherwood Forest with his wife and children. When he's not day-dreaming about Martian landscapes, he teaches creative writing and art.

PETRA

Petra was the first to discover winter. At least that's what she told me. Like every sweaty, shiny afternoon since the Landing, she was making her way home from college. As she always did. But this day, on some whim, she decided to leave the ordered rows of prefab homes and cut through the Prospect.

She strolled across the sloping lawns and scented flowerbeds, past children playing in the fountains and old timers basking like turtles, till she came to a quiet clutch of maples. There, as she was about to sit and read her study notes, she saw it. A maple dappled not in green but flaming yellow. Not one wilting leaf but the entire canopy. As she looked around at the beautiful contagion spreading from tree to tree, her body shuddered.

It would be inspiring to think this was true, in the light of later events. Of course it was impossible to prove, because soon half of Calsillas was aware. The line of gold and ochre crept across the continental forests like bushfire. TV crews even followed its progression on their bulletins.

Within days a second dilemma dawned on the public consciousness. The hours of daylight were getting shorter, just a second or so per day, but enough to spark panic. Daylight shrinkage, as it was called, became a national obsession. Protest rallies were organised outside the Government Complex, calling for 'a fair day's light for a fair day's work'.

'People of Calsillas,' the Senator Prime announced on live teleview. 'As your elected leader, I will do everything in my power to bring about a full restoration of daylight. Nor will I rest until every tree on the planet has grown new leaves. To this end, I have ordered Jackson University to focus their best brains on a strategy, with unlimited Treasury support.'

Which was how I came to meet Petra.

The University called a campus-wide interdepartmental plenary. The idea was to fine-tune their conclusions before going public.

I arrived deliberately late, pushing through the doors into a lecture hall tinged with the odour of lunchtime curry. Academics from every faculty crammed together on the stage while the auditorium was a sea of anxious youth.

I grabbed the only remaining seat, beside an intense-looking girl. Her eyes were dark, almost black, and her hair a neglected mess of chestnut curls. Her skin was pale, as though she'd never stepped outside the library. But when she flashed me an awkward smile, her face burned with intelligence. This was Petra.

I glanced up at the holographic sphere spinning above the auditorium, a facsimile of Calsillas, and whispered, 'What have I missed?'

She gave me a look of impatience and answered, 'Shifting polar axis equals unstable orbit equals global cooling and the end of the world, got it?'

I nodded, mustered an expression of gravitas and turned my attention to the bearded scholars at the front. A geeky boy in the first row was asking a question.

'But is this winter thing really so bad, Sir? Can't we simply adapt our crops to cooler weather?'

Professor Gortin, the wizened old head of Meteorology, shook his head sadly. 'Young man, this is only what I term "pre-winter", a season of change before the impending apocalypse. True winter, when it arrives, will be nothing but snow and darkness. We'll freeze.'

A chorus of gasps flowed through the assembly.

A podgy girl with pigtails waved her hand. 'Why don't we just fly away like our ancestors?'

Dr. Bukolov glared at the girl through horn-rimmed spectacles. 'I see now why you flunked Astrophysics 101. There's no way we'd have the resources to build spaceships for two million people. No, we must stand our ground, stand or fall.'

The audience broke into a babble. Professor Ekk, the Vice Chancellor, took to his feet and bellowed, 'Silence!' His huge girth and flowing silver mane made an imposing sight and a hush descended on the room.

'Our combined brilliance has devised a plan.' He aimed a remote at the spinning orb. Curtains of iridescent colour gushed from both axes. 'The rotational pole has slipped its tether and wanders freely, causing this climatic calamity.'

The Professor paused, casting a baleful look around his tight-lipped audience. 'First, we find the original East Pole, the one true Orient. We set off an ion flare, the most powerful ever built. This will interact with Calsillas' magnetosphere, realigning the pole, and putting an end to these gravitational wobbles.'

I leaned over to Petra, glad of an excuse to make conversation, and whispered in her ear, 'What's a magneto thingummy?'

She sniffed. 'The magnetic field. It surrounds the planet and shields us from the solar radiation. Look it up on the Cal-web.'

'Oh that,' I replied, as knowingly as I could.

Petra ignored me and instead leant forward in her seat. 'Sir, is there to be an expedition to the Eastern Wastes?' she asked.

The distinguished gentleman nodded.

A tall girl at the back, with long blond hair and immaculate teeth, held up her arm. 'What about the Spectres? They say the ravines there are haunted.'

A wave of titters surfed around the room and the girl blushed beetroot.

The Head of Classical Studies took to his feet. 'Our ancestors were forever populating the wildernesses of Earth with imaginary folk creatures, my dear. Abominable snowmen, fairies, sea monsters, et cetera. Man continues this silly habit as he crawls through the Milky Way. There are no monsters on Calsillas, nor any life whatsoever before Humanity arrived three centuries ago.'

An overwhelming urge grabbed hold of me and I sprang up. 'After all, if anything did exist in the Eastern Wastes, it would have been spotted by a prospector decades ago.'

Two hundred pairs of eyes fixed directly on me. My legs buckled and I collapsed backwards.

Petra glowed with a look of approval. 'Hear, hear,' she said. 'Academia is no place for superstition.'

Professor Ekk drew himself up to his full and considerable height. 'On the boards outside, we've posted a list for volunteers. Think carefully before committing yourself. It's going to be a long, arduous trek. On the other hand, how many graduates can put "Saving Humanity" on their resumé?'

He had scarcely spat out the last syllable before the room erupted in a mass scrum for the exits. Everyone, apparently, wanted to be a hero.

Petra and I breezed out on to the top of the steps. The campus panned out in all directions, white prefabs set among cherry groves. The former pinks and burgundies of blossom had been replaced by brown crackly leaves. Great drifts clogged up the nooks of the faculty buildings. The wind caught the stragglers and lifted them high into the monotone sky.

'It's depressing, isn't it,' she remarked, pulling up the collar of her coat.

'I kind of like it.'

She stared at me oddly.

'You signed up. I saw you,' I said. 'Do you think you'll be chosen?'

She flashed me that intense smile. 'They'll have to take me.'

'You sound confident.'

'I designed the software for the flare.' She gave a little pout and my lungs breathed harder. Then she started down the steps, across the leaf-littered turf.

I gave chase. 'Could you put in a good word for me?'

Petra stopped, as though I had uttered the most absurd thing. 'What have you got to offer? What's your major? '

I hung my head. 'Um - Sports and Leisure studies.' Glancing up, I expected a derisive laugh.

Instead, Petra looked pitying. 'Hardly a prerequisite for an academic mission.'

'Oh really, Einstein? Who carries all that heavy gear then? Can't see you doing hard labour.'

She shrugged. 'Good point! Any other skills to mention?' She cast an eye over my torso, and then, ever so slightly, reddened.

'I assume the trip will set sail from Eastport? My home town. A touch of local knowledge always comes in handy.'

'Guess so.' She thought for a moment. 'Why haven't I seen you around?'

Now it was my turn to blush, to the roots of my hair. 'New boy. Just transferred from Eastport Tech.'

Her perfect forehead creased into a frown. She seemed to be grasping for something. Whatever it was, the frown evaporated and she beamed. 'I'll see what I can do. Your name?'

'Victor, Victor Kassily.' I gave a deep bow.

Petra held back a giggle. 'Well, Victor Kassily, I go this way. Good day.' She gestured towards the postgraduate apartments and broke into a trot.

'Wait up!' I cried, and caught her by the arm. This startled her and I cursed myself.

She raised an exquisite eyebrow.

'Would you like me to walk you home? We can talk about the mission, if you want?'

'No, thank you,' she replied, in a wavering voice. 'I'm fine.'

Things got off to a bad start and went downhill from there. When our vehicle turned into the Eastport docks, the "Save Our Winter" protestors were out in force. These young, idealistic rejects had banded together to support one cause - namely, that winter was a natural phenomenon, as much a part of the planet's ecosystem as the mountains and oceans. They referred to themselves as the Winter Guard.

'Idiots!' Professor Ekk blasted from the front seat, spitting out great globules of saliva.

The protestors battered the windows with their fists, shrieking slogans.

'Hands off our planet!'

'Keep Calsillas natural!'

Petra buried her face in her hands.

I was in the opposite seat, and placed my hand on her arm. 'They can't stop you.'

'What about these rumours? That the Winter Guard are going to wage some kind of terrorist campaign against us?'

I smirked. 'Crackpots! They couldn't catch apples on a windy day.'

Petra stared into my eyes, seeking something which wasn't there.

I turned away from her laser beam gaze.

'Perhaps,' she replied thoughtfully, putting her hand around mine and squeezing it. My pulse broke into a sprint.

That night the first accident happened. The robocrane was hoisting a crate of equipment on to our cargo-sized ship, *The Star of the Orient*, when the ropes snapped. The box crashed and splintered, killing two of our team. But with a chilly breeze and the sun setting absurdly early, Professor Ekk announced there was no time for grieving. We slipped moorings and set sail.

Our passage took us across The New Gandhi Straits, the name a reflection of its peaceful reputation.

On the second day, the tides boiled, whipping up mountainous waves and gale force winds. Night fell, hardly distinguishable from the vast swell of black water. The storm toyed with *The Star*, heaving it up like driftwood, only to send it plummeting into the pit of each wave.

Below decks everyone had taken to their cabins. I stalked the shadows, listening to the groans from behind each door. The stink of vomit clung to the air.

Almost by chance I found myself exactly where I wanted to be. 'It's Victor, can I come in?'

Petra called out 'yes' and, caught by a wave, I stumbled into her cabin.

Her tiny room was bare and reeked of the last passenger's perspiration. I collapsed into the nailed-down chair, with Petra beside me on the bunk. We were so close I could feel her breath on my face. She seemed impressively immune from the seasickness.

'The trick is not to think about it,' she said, with a trace of a smile.

'The nausea?'

She nodded.

'Aw, I got my sea legs long ago, on my first voyage,' I explained.

'You've sailed before?'

'Oh, sure, with my father. He was a prospector.'

'So, you've already been to the Eastern Wastes?'

'No, never, only up coast,' I replied quickly.

'Pity. You could've come in useful.'

Her voice had that scathing edge to it. I was coming to like it.

She lapsed into silence. Moments turned into minutes, all the time the cabin swinging like a roller coaster. Another storm was raging inside my skull. Thoughts crashed into each other, emotions bubbled, memories howled.

I glanced at Petra, brave and steadfast. An image of her frozen-eyed corpse flitted through my imagination. My brain raced. There had to be a way to save her? Somewhere in all this fury, my body overwhelmed my intellect.

A gigantic wave threw me on to the bed. I grabbed her roughly and forced a kiss. I hated my clumsiness, a barbarian before a goddess, but I knew no other way. She pushed me back. My hands seized her shoulders.

'Before it's too late. Please.'

Like a melting glacial wall, her reserve shattered. She pressed her lips on to mine and we embraced.

In the belly of the tempest, we made love. The sea rocked and heaved, throwing us against each other. I was the tornado, battering her unblemished shore. And then we broke, exhausted and clinging to each other like debris.

The rains pummelled the hull, a moment of tranquillity, the eye of the storm.

That moment passed. Petra shifted away from me, as if my flesh suddenly repelled her.

'Go,' she whispered, through tears.

The sea was a millpond when we sailed into the primitive harbour of Hard Welcome. It was not until disembarkation that three students were discovered missing.

'Youth today!' Professor Ekk bemoaned. 'Fancy puking your guts over the side without taking a firm grip of the railings! They'll get posthumous firsts, naturally. '

Hard Welcome made Eastport seem metropolitan. A handful of prefabs fanned out around the pier. The countryside was a cold desert and unbearably flat, save for some pale hills that streaked the far-off horizon.

One solitary hotel loomed over the port. We checked in for the night. At dinner time we ventured into the hotel's fly-stained restaurant.

Two scrawny waiters ferried out plates of jellied fish, alongside a boiled lobster the size of a dog. No one else noticed its odd aroma, and I said nothing, quietly opting for the canned items on the menu.

Petra deliberately sat at the opposite end of the table to me. After lights out, I knocked on her door.

'I want to be alone, Victor.'

My heart strained for explanation, why she had cried, why she was pushing me away. But common sense overruled, the mission was too important. I bit my tongue and sloped off to a lonely bedroom.

In the morning, five members of our party were too ill to get up, two lecturers and three of the undergraduates. The only doctor in town, a shrivelled up man stinking of whisky, was hastily summoned.

'Food poisoning. Probably the lobster,' he announced to the rest of us in the draughty lobby. 'They won't be fit for a week.'

Professor Ekk paced the floorboards, his enormous shape towering over our heads.

'Overnight frosts have been reported in the Far West. We must press on. We're down to a skeleton crew, but we can do it.'

'Wouldn't it be advisable to wait?' Petra interrupted.

He fished in his pocket and pulled out a silver, circular gadget with an ornate base, which he held out on the chubby palm of his hand. A dial with a graded circumference spun clockwise, then anticlockwise.

'Some kind of antique watch?' one of the boys asked.

Petra sniffed. 'It's an antique, alright, but a compass, not a watch.'

'Very good,' Ekk said, in a calmer tone. 'My ancestors brought this from Earth, works by good old-fashioned magnetism. It must be two thousand years old, if it's a day. I've adjusted it for Calsillas.'

The yo-yoing dial came to rest, with the letter E marked in red, pointing towards the hinterland.

The Professor stroked his beard. 'Ah, true magnetic East! Let's not lose heart, my dear young things. Destiny is riding on our shoulders, ours and ours alone.'

An hour later the two lumo-vans set off and Hard Welcome disappeared into the dust from our wheels.

I sat alone in the rear of the larger vehicle, surrounded by the machinery which would make the ionic flare. With my limited knowledge of science, this was an opportunity to study the gizmos up close, and maybe get some idea of how it would all work. Knowledge which might prove vital to the success of my plan.

A youth called Demidov crawled back to join me. I summoned up my best imitation of a friendly smile.

At only eighteen, he was the youngest of our party, but an engineering genius apparently. His hair was an unruly brown mess, and his pink face spotted with pimples.

'Do you think it's the Winter Guard?' he began, his baby-blue eyes gleaming with fear.

I grunted a 'What?'

'Seems we've been ill-fated from the get go. One calamity after another.'

I stared out of the grimy window at the never-ending, stone-grey flatness.

'Sabotage? Nah, we've had some bad luck, perhaps, but it's behind us now. I'm sure.'

The anxious look on his blubbery face deepened.

'Do you believe in ghosts, Victor Kassily?'

I laughed.

'Seriously,' he went on. 'I mean the Spectres of legend. Supposing they really existed and were casting some kind of jinx on us?'

'Call yourself a scientist? Three million years since Homo Sapiens first ventured from his cave. And in all those eons has he ever found proof of a ghost, or a witch, or bogeyman?'

But Demidov did not look reassured. 'I'm keeping my eyes peeled, brother. Whether it's the Winter Guard or the Spectres, either way I'll stop them.'

'Ok, I'll let you know if I see anything suspicious.'

A childlike smile spread across his lips and he patted me on the back.

With dusk dropping fast from the highlands, we stopped and set up camp, a half dozen tents flapping between the two lumo-vans.

I came across Petra, leaning against the bonnet of the smaller vehicle, her pretty face framed in a circle of fox-coloured fur. She was watching the sun melt into the northern horizon. The air was laced with an icy, dry sharpness.

She glanced at me and shivered. 'Doesn't it seem unnatural?'

I gave a bewildered shrug. She went on, 'Darkness falling at six in the evening? It's bizarre!'

'Didn't Earth have long nights?' I replied, desperate for any chance to talk to her. She stuck out her lower lip. 'How prehistoric. '

She pushed past me and zipped herself into her tent. A voice inside my head urged me to follow, but she was lost to me now. Why, I didn't know, but there was no point obsessing about it.

I kicked the mudguard on the lumo-van. My toes tingled with pain, bringing my senses into sharp focus. The fate of Calsillas was what mattered, not some capricious young woman.

In the morning Demidov's tent was open and deserted. A handwritten note pinned to the canvas stated that we were all cursed and he had decided to head back to Hard Welcome.

'On foot? Is that boy barking mad?' Ekk thundered to the remaining six of us.

Gloomily, we went about the morning tasks. Chains were fitted to the lumo-vans and we began the final leg, the ascent to the plateau. The slope rose above the desert in fits and starts. Some of the ascending contours were smooth, eroded by eons of wind. Others were jagged, like the bones of fossilised behemoths.

For over an hour the lumo-vans inched higher, their chains clinging precariously to the steep angle. My stomach churned with every jolt, but at length our vehicles drove on to the summit. Everyone broke into a cheer. We'd made it!

'So much for the curse,' Ekk mumbled sulkily from the front passenger seat.

Petra, who was sitting behind him, caught my eye. 'That's pure superstition, isn't it, Victor?' she asked, determinedly.

Beyond the window a tableland panned out in all directions, an endless plateau littered with boulders and gravel. The sky formed a perfect dome, blue and cloudless. The warmth and home comforts of civilisation seemed a long way away.

'Looks like glacial formation,' Ekk remarked, scrutinising the bleak landscape.

'But Professor, doesn't that mean there have been long winters before?' I asked.

'Presumably, but it's this one we have to worry about.'

Never a truer word spoken.

'We've found it!' Ekk tossed his ancient compass back to Petra. She held it up and gasped. The dial was spinning crazily.

'True magnetic East.' Her voice squeaked with excitement.

I scanned the exterior. What was so special about this scrap of land? It could have been some barren moon, or any one of the galaxy's lifeless worlds. I thought of the ravines beyond this tabletop, with their labyrinth of gullies and fissures. This place was a dead zone in comparison.

Nevertheless, our arrival lifted the crew's spirits. They leapt out into the rarefied air and set to work. All day they hammered away. Bolts were tightened, fuel cells loaded and pipes connected. The ion gun took shape, an elongated cylinder studded with plasma coils, one end pointing to the heavens, the other piercing deep into the topsoil. Its black, metallic surface gleamed in the frigid sunshine

32

and put me in mind of an evil robot, waiting for some foolish scientist to switch it on.

By evening the structure was almost complete. Ekk, whose face had aged a decade in one afternoon, ordered us to down tools. We clambered into the lumo-vans and drove a safe distance from the gun's radioactive core.

Although there was a lot to do, my muscles cried out for rest. I quickly put up my tent, slipped into the thermal bag and surrendered to oblivion....

The pale dawn found a new colour. Red. The barren dust was soaked in it. I hesitated outside Petra's tent, my mind a battlefield. But when I pulled down the zip, she was gone. Relief filled me. Then dismay chased away that euphoria as I realised she could only be one place - the ion gun! I strained for a glimpse across the plateau. The only thing I could see was the distant ion gun, like a blade of onyx piercing the dull, heavy clouds.

I ran, leaping craters and rocks. 'STOP!'

Petra stood beside the control panel, typing in the activation protocols. Her fingers flew across the keyboard with dazzling speed. But then she hesitated, pulled something from inside her fur coat and aimed it at me. A pistol.

I halted so abruptly I tumbled, gashing my knee on a boulder. 'Where did you get that?' I cried, nursing my injury.

She glared a look which made me want to cry.

'From the Professor. He wouldn't believe me, though. Don't think that's down to your skills as an infiltrator. His moon-sized ego couldn't accept he'd been fooled. Still, he gave me this.'

I shifted on to my knees. 'Please, stop, the ion gun's going to kill you.'

She snorted and, with her free hand, continued tapping the keys, her gaze darting between the console and me.

'I'm telling the truth. The flare is programmed to explode. You'll be blown apart.'

Her face was a mask of loathing. Any love she might have felt was gone. Anguish filled me, as though my heart was about to burst through my ribcage.

The control panel flickered, followed by a soft whirring. The ion gun was charging. This would take a few minutes. Was it enough time to save her? I stood up.

'Stay still,' she barked. 'I'll use it, I will.'

I nodded. 'Let me explain.'

She gestured with the pistol to the red stains on my thermal jacket. 'That's the only explanation I need.'

A hush fell between us. I looked around at the pall seeping across the landscape.

'When did you rumble me?' I asked at last.

She considered for a moment. 'From the very first meeting there was something not quite right. A nagging doubt at the back of my mind, then a suspicion. Yesterday I looked at you, and somehow it all fitted together. So I left camp early. Nothing's going to stop this flare going off. Not even a traitor.'

Guilt drowned me. Yes, I'd done terrible things, but I had the best of motives. And yet I'd lost Petra.

'It was me, alright. The robocrane, those students overboard, the poison-laced lobster.'

'And Demidov?'

'I lured him out to the boulders and bashed in his teenage skull.'

Petra clicked the trigger. Tears were transforming her eyes into pools of dark beauty. She was close to shooting, but couldn't do it in cold blood. Not Petra.

'I crept into every tent, cutting their throats while they slept. But when I found you gone, I was glad. I want you to live, Petra.'

The pistol was trembling in her hand.

'You've killed them? Everyone?'

An image of the late Professor Ekk pushed into my mind, of a fat stupid man, awaking to see cascading ribbons of his own blood. And the knife in my hand.

'Yes.'

'For your stupid campaign?'

I frowned. 'Oh, you mean the Winter Guard?' I laughed, shuffling nearer.

'You think this is amusing, Victor?'

'No, of course not. But I'm nothing to do with those idiots.'

Her exquisite eyebrows arched in bewilderment.

'The Spectres sent me.'

For a split second her aim wavered. Should I rush her? Then she steadied her grip. 'What are you talking about?'

I glanced about us, at the odd, impenetrable cloud mass gathering overhead, at the surrounding bleak plateau, an entire world magnificently stripped of colour.

'Sixty years ago, I accompanied my father on one of his hare-brained trips. Into the ravines beyond this stumpy mountain.'

'And you in your twenties? Can't you honour my intelligence with a worthy lie?'

'Listen, Petra. My father was a prospector. Always scouring the Wastes for gold or uranium, anything that could turn lift us from poverty. A fool. He stumbled off a ledge and by the time I reached him - '

The long ago memory of my father, with bones twisted and eyes empty as glass, burned through me. 'I wandered for days, hopelessly lost. Eventually I collapsed, waited for the end. But they saved me. '

'They?'

I marvelled at how her voice could make a single syllable sound so perfect.

'Ekk got it so totally, utterly wrong. Winter is a natural part of Calsillas, not an aberration. The seasons last for millennia here, not months, like on Earth. The Spectres are a winter people. They thrive in the ice age, and then hibernate through centuries of sunshine.'

'Lies!'

'All true. My presence disturbed *Garathrill*, my new father. He left their underground chambers and found me. Took me back and made me hibernate. You see, the hibernation is a kind of communal dreaming. They pass eons of dreaded summertime in a dreamscape. And they absorbed me into that dream. I spent decades sleeping, while their power healed my outer body. We call it *t'narrak*, the energy which nurtures.'

Petra's cheeks were as grey as the surrounding stones. 'I don't believe…'

I took a step closer. The whirring was getting louder.

'You should see the dreamscape. A life more wonderful than reality. But now it's winter, and my people are rousing to claim back their planet. And the things they do with ice, Petra, whole cities hewn from ice caps and polished like marble, dazzling spires, arching highways, glistening fields of snow.'

'SHUT UP!'

'Petra, humanity is the usurper. But we had the perfect weapon. Victor Kassily! They sent me to spy. When I discovered what your university was up to, I had to prevent it. I wasn't even enrolled. Yes, I faked that too. If summer doesn't end, the Spectres won't wake up. The *t'narrak* is running out. It's time for them to live, otherwise they'll fade away.'

'But, Victor, we'll die. We can't survive never-ending winter.'

I looked at my blood-stained boots. 'That's not my problem. You could live on, with me. There's a way. Please, Petra, will you?'

The shot rang out, like a peel of thunder. I felt the searing heat as the bullet whistled past my ear.

'Does that answer your obscene proposal?' she hissed, through gritted teeth.

The charging of the ion flare was nearly complete. Last night, while the scientists were having the weak shoddy dreams of humans, I'd reprogrammed the containment chamber to flood. Not bad for a Sports and Leisure undergraduate. Except, of course, I was nothing of the sort.

The Dreaming had given me a long time to learn, about technology, about many things. Not so much about love, perhaps, but none of that mattered now. Petra was standing at the epicentre of the coming blast.

'Petra, I love you.'

Funny how words have effect. Petra stared at me, mouth gaping, unwittingly lowering the pistol. I threw myself upon her. Even as she raised her arm, fury written across her porcelain features, we collided. I shoved with all my might. Something about finality gives you strength.

Her everlasting eyes stared into mine as she tripped backwards. The ion gun was behind me. I never heard the explosion. A blinding light and plumes of smoke swallowed me. I crashed face down.

Strangely, the pain was bearable. Shock does that, I guess. Just a stinging sensation from my neck to my buttocks, where my back used to be.

I managed to roll over, on to my side. You see, even the wonders of the Spectres' Dreaming had nothing on what I was about to witness. Petra, staggering to her feet, bruised and bleeding, but alive. She was screaming something, but the blast had blown out my eardrums. I'd like to think it was protestations of love.

Which would have been enough, but there was more. White flakes glistening upon those perfect cheekbones. So beautiful. I sunk backwards, on to the exposed knuckles of my vertebrae. The pain intensified, rockets of agony blasting off inside my skull.

I didn't care. My eyes were full of the dark clouds above.

And there it came, drifting down towards me - the first flurry of snow.

GARY EVERINGTON has spent most of his childhood in York and Liverpool.

As a young man, he trained as a teacher and then taught for several years in London Boroughs before being appointed to a headship in Hertfordshire. It was while training for the profession that he met his wife, Alison. They have two children and four grandchildren.

Gary enjoys writing across a range of genres and this, together with his many other interests, fills his time.

He is now retired and lives in Hemel Hempstead.

REALITY CHECK

To the scientists at CERN
and all the High Priests of this world

If you are reading this, then my insignificant life is over. I have left no mark on the world, but I do have a story to tell. It is an account of something which happened many years ago when I was young and thought I could see clearly.

The fog of old age and approaching death grows thicker but the memory of those few days still burns bright. Like a pebble tossed into a small pond, I share it with you. Perhaps the ripples it will cause will move outwards and build into waves. The shore line of ultimate truth awaits their arrival.

I am out of reach of mockery and ridicule but you are not. So take my small piece of puzzle and handle it with care until you can find where it fits in creation's jigsaw.

My life was of little consequence. I was merely an observer who witnessed something extraordinary. Even as I write, I wonder if I was deceived or simply mistaken.

In two thousand and eleven, I was working as a junior physicist at CERN. I was surprised to have been given such a prestigious placement, my scientific achievements being mediocre at best. However, it was soon apparent my academic ability was of little consequence. My sponsors expected no more of me than routine work, assisting senior colleagues.

One particular scientist was of interest to my sponsors. It soon became clear my true role was to follow him, both in his work and his private moments.

How anyone is seduced into becoming a spy is an interesting lesson in human frailty. I was easily seduced; spying takes little effort and pays well.

Who my true sponsors were and what their interest was must remain a mystery. This is not out of any sense of loyalty on my part. I simply do not know.

They say genius is close to madness and, in the case of Gustav Erickson, this was certainly true. He was the madman in the mix; tolerated because his ramblings and flights of fantasy might just trigger something new.

You need people like him at the frontiers of science. Someone who lets their imagination fly, unfettered by pre-conceived ideas or common knowledge. After all, Einstein said, *'Logic will get you from A to B but imagination will get you everywhere.'*

There were two incidents at CERN during my time there which I believe pushed Gustav over the edge.

The first was when, after long months of experiments and data analysis, it was declared that no evidence of the Higgs Boson particle had been found in the expected mass range. The God particle remained hidden or did not exist at all.

This spurred Gustav into a burst of hyper-activity. You would catch him wandering around the complex muttering, 'It can't be found if it is not there. I told them it wasn't there.'

He would disappear into his room and emerge days later clutching wads of calculations. He would thrust these under the noses of anyone careless enough to be cornered.

A few, out of curiosity or kindness, perused his work, only to conclude the equations they contained were so complex as to be almost impossible to follow or check.

He claimed he was near to developing a new aspect of string theory which would at last tie gravity into the Standard Model.

Unkindly, his colleagues referred to his embryonic theory as 'Two strings and three elastic bands'.

The second incident happened a few months later when CERN went public on a whole series of experiments seemingly showing subatomic particles travelling faster than light.

The implications reverberated around the scientific world and resonated with whatever was inside Gustav's head. Suddenly everything was in the melting pot. If the constant used in almost every calculation in particle physics proved not constant, then all our grand theories were worth nothing. Or, in common parlance, perhaps we had got hold of the wrong end of the stick.

Gustav's behaviour became extreme.

One day I found him with his head pressed against the outer casing of the Hadron collider. I asked him what he was doing.

Before I continue, I ought to explain. I recorded as faithfully as possible every conversation I had with him. At the time, it was nothing more than what was required by my paymasters and I thought little of it. It took only a small measure of discipline, the kind one needs to write a daily diary.

It is only afterwards I came to realise how valuable these conversations may turn out to be. It is just possible within these words lies the answer.

I therefore reproduce them as they happened.

'What are you doing Gustav?' I asked

'They are in my head, Peter. In my head, going round faster and faster.'

'What are?'

'All of them.'

'All of them?'

'All the bits of stuff we get when we smash things together.'

'You mean quarks, leptons, bosons?'

'Yes, there all there in my head, except for the Higgs, of course. It doesn't exist.'

'I don't understand, Gustav ... they can't actually be in your head; not as separate entities.'

He gave me a withering look. 'I know... idiot.' He turned away and carried on the conversation with himself. 'The Higgs does not exist, so what is the force that gives them mass and where is the graviton hiding?'

Gustav was becoming a nuisance, so much so he was politely but forcefully asked to take a week off. Surprisingly, he accepted willingly, exclaiming he needed time to clear the clutter from his head. I was lucky, I was owed a week's holiday and I quickly arranged to take it.

CERN held several properties set in beautiful surroundings within thirty miles of the complex. These were used to host visiting dignitaries or as retreats for the overworked staff.

It was to one of these places, set high in the mountains above Lake Tanay, that Gustav and I went. He was not pleased to discover my presence but the luxurious catered chalet was big enough for us to maintain our distance, if so inclined, and Gustav made it quite clear that was his intention.

Nothing happened of any note for two days. Gustav spent most of this time sitting on the balcony, staring into space. He did not read or listen to music. There was a TV in the lounge and each of the bedrooms but I never saw or heard him use them. He simply sat and stared. Occasionally he would stand, walk aimlessly about and then slap his head.

Only once did I try to engage him in conversation. He was sitting in the lounge. His eyes were closed but he was clearly awake as the fingers of both hands were drumming on the arms of the chair.

'Are you ok, Gustav?' I asked.

He opened his eyes and stared at me. 'It's like I am a blind man, Peter; a blind man sitting in his own lounge. He thinks he knows all the contents of the room and understands exactly where they are. He can fumble his way around and live comfortably but he is unhappy. Unhappy because he knows there is something else in the room. Something beyond his knowledge, something all around him yet it remains elusive. He is unhappy because he knows if he could, just for a moment, grasp the elusive something then everything would become clear.'

He paused and closed his eyes again. His fingers resumed their drumming. With his eyes closed and his fingers tapping, he continued as much to himself as to me.

'For the blind man, the elusive something is light. I am the blind man but, for me, it is not light that is missing, it is something else; there is something there, just out of reach. It is teasing me. If only I could grasp it for just a second then I would understand and fly with the gods.'

The next morning Gustav arrived at breakfast, dressed for walking. Fortunately, I had surfaced early and had almost finished eating. This gave me plenty of time to return to my room and don similar attire. This was more like what I had expected.

On several occasions in the past, Gustav had headed for the mountains. He would spend a day or two walking in the high pastures and return revitalised. I knew from experience following him would be difficult.

Above the treeline, you can see for miles. All he had to do was look back and he would spot me. I decided I would follow from a distance, hoping if he turned I would not be recognised and he would assume I was a fellow walker.

In the event, my concern was misplaced. He took a trail leading upwards and set a relentless pace I found hard to match. He was attacking the mountain with the same determination and energy he displayed in his work and I was left floundering in his wake.

Not once did he look back or pause to take in the view. After an hour of hard climbing, he disappeared between a mass of boulders and jagged outcrops. Not wanting to lose him, I made an effort to quicken my pace.

We were somewhere on the ridge. Hundreds of feet below, to my right, I saw Lake Tanay glistening in the morning sun. Of Gustav, there was no sign. The path had disintegrated into a scramble over frost-shattered rocks. Some towered above me like giant teeth set in the jawline that was the crest of the ridge.

I made my way gingerly across a tricky section, conscious of the sheer drop on my right and, on my left, something as close to sheer as to make no difference. I picked my way round a large outcrop and almost bumped into Gustav.

He was less than fifteen metres away, standing on a spur of rock which jutted out of the mountainside. The rock and Gustav seemed suspended in space. Above was a brilliant blue sky dotted with cotton wool clouds while, on three sides and below, there was nothing but a heart stopping one thousand foot drop. He was standing perfectly still, staring upwards.

I followed his gaze, wondering what he was looking at. Two birds circled effortlessly above, their large outspread wings almost motionless. As I watched, one dipped to the side and slid silently through the air, losing hundreds of feet in seconds. The second bird followed until both were at a similar altitude. They flew in giant circles until, suddenly, finding an up current they climbed, riding the thermal like a giant invisible elevator.

I sat down behind two rocks, positioning myself so I could observe and not be seen. I must have been sitting there for at least five minutes while Gustav stood and watched the birds.

A sound from somewhere beyond him drew both our attention. Two men appeared from behind an outcrop. They must have climbed up to the crest from the other side. Gustav acknowledged their arrival with a slight raising of his hand and immediately went back to watching the birds.

The two men sat on a rock, took out water bottles and drank. They sat in silence, watching Gustav and the birds.

Eventually one of the men placed his water flask on the ground, stood, and made his way out on to the spur of rock where Gustav was standing. He approached cautiously. It was not a good place to startle anyone.

Gustav heard, or felt, the man's presence and turned. I was surprised to see him smile in greeting. The walk and birdwatching had done him good.

'Penny for you thoughts?' said the man.

'Not worth that much,' replied Gustav, with a hint of genuine despondency.

'Try me,' the man responded.

'I was watching the birds, envying their complete mastery of their environment; I was wishing I could fly free, like them.'

'What's stopping you?'

Gustav smiled and peered cautiously over the edge before turning back.

'Just the little matter of gravity.'

'That shouldn't stop you. After all, gravity is hardly a force, more a warping of space time, isn't it?'

It was a question asked in the same tone of voice as used by experienced teachers worldwide; an interesting mixture of challenge, kindness and confident self-knowledge with a hint of amusement added for good measure.

Gustav stared at his companion. It was the kind of response he might have expected from someone in the corridors of the complex. Coming from Joe Public, on top of a mountain, it surprised him.

'Are you a physicist?'

The man threw back his head and chuckled, his mass of tightly curled blond hair shaking.

'No...not a physicist ....'

Gustav instantly homed in on the slight hint of mockery in the man's reply.

'What's wrong with physicists?'

'Nothing's wrong with them…they amuse me… they lock themselves away in vast underground chambers and literally go round in circles hunting for something that is staring them in the face all the time.'

Gustav was hooked, and so was I.

'What do you mean? What is staring them in the face?'

The man paused for a moment and looked away as if considering something important. He made his decision and turned back to Gustav. 'Tell me, Gustav. How did the universe begin?'

Reader, let me draw your attention to something that went unnoticed by Gustav. The man had used his name. Yet at no point had names been exchanged. The man knew who Gustav was.

Gustav was eminently qualified to answer the question. He could have described in detail the explosion of the primeval atom and subsequent events on a timescale measured in nano seconds or billions of years.

As it was, he kept it simple.

'With the Big Bang!'

'Wrong! That is what came next.'

Gustav was shocked

'You mean before the Big Bang?'

The man nodded. 'Just before.'

Gustav shook his head. 'We don't know. '

'Then let me tell you, Gustav. A single thought; a thought that crystallised out from the thought field spread uniformly throughout this universe and every other universe.'

Gustav stared at the man, his mouth slightly open. I could see him struggling with what he had heard. Then, in a voice not much more than a whisper, he asked, 'What was the thought?'

'Let there be light,' came the reply.

Gustav shrugged his shoulders dismissively. 'You mean God.'

The man shook his head. 'No, God did not arrive until much later. You are being trapped into describing something in terms of what you already know. A thought can crystallise out by nothing more than random circumstances. Once crystallised, the thought creates a certain reality. That reality is only maintained if it is observed and therefore reinforced by other thoughts holding the same pattern. Otherwise, it decays into the constant flux of the thought field.'

The man paused, letting Gustav digest what he had heard. After a few moments he continued. 'It became complicated when a random idea crystallised out and formed conscious beings. For the first time, the thought field constructs could be held static by constant observation. In addition, conscious beings, although they don't realise it, have the ability to manipulate the thought field. They can make crystals form. Each crystal a separate thought which then locks with other crystals forming a pattern which eventually becomes perceived as reality. Unknowingly, conscious beings created all sorts of things by simply imagining them.'

Gustav was far quicker than I was. He grasped both the content and the implication of what was being said.

'If that is true, then everything we see and understand is only held in place by our own collective thoughts.'

The man said nothing. He waited for Gustav to complete the logic trail. Gustav ticked off the evidence.

'So, the Higgs was not found because not enough people believed it was there; and perhaps God exists because enough people believe he does. That also explains why the observer alters the events of a quantum experiment by simply observing. It also explains the logic behind the anthropic principle.'

Gustav made the next jump.

'You mean, if someone believes something strongly enough, then that thought can change what we perceive as reality.'

The man nodded and smiled. 'Faith moves mountains or, perhaps in this case… gravity?'

Gustav paused and ran his fingers through his hair. From my hiding place, I could hear his breath rasping, almost panting in his throat. 'Are you saying that if I really believe I can fly, then I will?'

The man nodded. 'If you really believe and have no doubts in your head, you will fly. You will create a bubble of a different reality about you. It has been done before.'

Gustav looked up. 'It has? By whom?'

'What is magic if not the creation of a different reality? Alternatively, consider the miracles much loved by those of a more religious bent. Purely a matter of manipulating reality. Once, there were many magicians and miracle workers. As time goes by, the pattern becomes more set, more reinforced by increasing numbers of observers, but... it is still possible. Wasn't it Albert Einstein who said, *"There are two ways to live: you can live as if nothing is a miracle; you can live as if everything is a miracle"*.'

Gustav stepped away from the man and turned so that he could look across the valley. He stretched out his arms high above his head and yelled at the top of his voice. 'I was blind and now I see.'

With appalling certainty, I knew what was coming. Before I could yell or move, Gustav leapt into the void screaming, 'I can fly!'

Newtonian Physics is an adequate tool to help describe what happened. After one second, Gustav's body had fallen four point nine meters. By the end of the next second, this distance had increased to nineteen point six. Gustav's body accelerated until after approximately eight seconds it reached terminal velocity. That is the point where the acceleration, due to gravity, is matched by the body's drag due to air resistance. For a human body floundering about in free fall, this is approximately one hundred and twenty mph.

A few seconds later, Gustav's body smashed into what, for all intents and purposes, was an immovable object with a force of seven hundred and eighty-four Newtons. The result was entirely predictable.

You will understand I did not carry out these elementary calculations at the time; it was something I did later, in an attempt to hold on to a reality that I knew and understood. I can almost see you shrug your shoulders and hear you say, 'A sad story, but the fool simply threw himself off the edge while the balance of his mind was disturbed.' You would, of course, be repeating what many voiced in private, if not in public.

As to the manner of his passing, the coroner was kind and concluded, 'Death by misadventure.'

I did not declare that I had seen what happened, a decision apparently also made by the two men, for I never saw them again. It was difficult. He had not been pushed or even coerced into jumping; nothing would be gained by declaring my presence.

But I mislead both you and myself. It was not the fear of complicating matters or the embarrassment of revealing and explaining my covert presence which prevented me from speaking. For the true reason, we must return to the mountaintop and examine closely what followed.

You will also understand I was in shock, gripped by the horror of what I had witnessed. I have considered this over the years but am convinced, in spite of my emotional state, I was perfectly rational.

The blond curly haired man, peering over the edge, made a tutting sound as if disappointed with something, then turned and rejoined his colleague.

'What went wrong?' asked the other man.

He considered for a moment.

'He should have flown. He really did believe. Someone else's thoughts prevented the alternative reality bubble forming.'

They nodded in agreement. Together they walked out on to the spur, turned and stared at me. I was hidden between the rocks, with only a narrow crack through which I could see. Yet I am convinced they knew I was there. They were smiling.

Before I could react, they slowly rose into the air and moved gently out, over the abyss. They paused for a moment, suspended in space, their smiles mocking my disbelief. Then they accelerated upwards. I watched until they disappeared between the clouds.

So now you have it. There remain many unanswered questions. My entire life has been haunted by them.

Did I kill Gustav with my certainty he would fall?

Is this universe, and everything it contains, a pattern made from thoughts?

Did I imagine those two flying men?

If I did, does it make them any less real?

Look with objective eyes, sift the evidence and seek the truth.

But, be warned, for as our friend, Albert Einstein, said: *"Whoever undertakes to set himself up as a judge of Truth and Knowledge is shipwrecked by the laughter of the gods."*

JOHN GLANDER is an Obsessive Compulsive Writer. To him, writing is like breathing and eating, a necessity.

He began writing fiction at an early age and his first published piece was a story in a small magazine, followed by a number of stories published in limited circulation magazines; he then went on to edit a small magazine for a year.

There was a period when he was regularly publishing poetry in specialist magazines and had around seventy poems published. He also spent some time producing stage and audio plays, mostly with children's groups.

John writes stories for children and teens about adventure, mystery, a touch of magic, parallel worlds, riding and the problem with brothers, sisters, mothers and friends. For adults, the spread is similar with novels regarding contemporary life, slipstream novels, fantasy and future history.

MISTRESS OF HER TIME

'Miss Wilson, in this department we do have dress standards, so possibly a skirt rather longer, no studded collar or nose ring and perhaps it would be advisable to wear a more opaque blouse.'

'Plus, why don't you ditch the three hundred year old suit and float. Were you born old or did you need training?'

'Miss Wilson, a little respect, if you please.'

'I don't as it happens, Barry, my twitch. I shall say what I like and wear what I like. You need me too much to make a fuss.'

'May I point out you could still be returned to your cell where the process of law will resume its course.'

She glared at him. 'You mean you sell me to the Americans just because one of their people was brain dead enough to leave an open line into what they call their secrets. I tell you, my poisonous twitch, you'd find more interesting and intelligent stuff on the hard drive of a ten year old. Why you've got your head so far up their arses I don't know, unless it's a death wish.'

'Miss Wilson!'

'You need me to sort out your mess, though I tell you now it's none of your terrorists, not even the one you think has access to atomic materials and an organisation of thousands but really works for the Council in Bolton.'

'Seriously?' His attitude changed.

'Pick up! I tell you something else, whatever I find, you won't like it. This ain't someone tinkering or playing games. This little arrow could point where you don't like it, even at the people you think are friends. Look on the printer.'

'Why?'

'Your CIA file. What they really think of you.'

She felt it would stop him and allow her to get on with what she knew would be her greatest ever challenge. The trouble was the stupid twitch was right. She could be sent back to prison and they would ship her off to the Americans because they did it to anyone who used a computer to learn things their suits didn't like. The Americans wouldn't have spotted her if she'd wanted to get into their system.

Kat had found most security systems were comparatively easy to break into if you could think the way they thought. Everything was about mindsets. She had been in a few places because she had been bored and had wanted to prove to herself she could do it, but it had been years earlier.

After she had reached fifteen years old, she had stopped bothering. There had been other things to think about. She'd been at home at the time, well, what she called home. It was a little one and a half bedroom flat in the cellar of an old building. It wasn't damp, unless the weather was really bad, and while there were rats in the yard, they didn't get into the building. The few which tried were fried. Her method of stopping them was probably illegal, but there was no one who cared.

She didn't live in what was called a bad area, but they rarely saw any police. She had been really shaken when they had burst into the flat. They had no reason to knock down the door. She would have opened it, if she'd been able to get up and put something on.

Half a dozen men with big guns looking at her when she was completely naked was not a pleasant experience.

'What the hell do you lot want?'

A suit pushed his way through. 'Miss Wilson, you are under arrest pursuant to Section One Eight Three of the Patriot Act 2043 and Section Sixty-Two of the Misuse of Information Technology Act.'

'Those are American shit and this is England.'

'Same thing. You're coming with us. Oh, and put some clothes on.'

She couldn't argue. The man with the largest gun always won. The Americans were going downhill rapidly, which was why they'd stepped up the bullying. It was all they had left.

They had no legal rights to operate in

England but it had never bothered them and the government always looked the other way. She had no idea why they wanted her, and she couldn't work out how they had found her.

It wasn't what she thought. Kat had the idea she was actually in a police station, though it wouldn't have been the local one. She had been taken far enough to be somewhere in central London.

'Right!' She was chained to a chair in front of a desk in an ill-lit room, like in the old crime dramas, only she didn't think anyone else knew they weren't real. 'We want the names of your associates and who you were feeding the information to. Go easier on you if you co-operate.'

She knew she was in deep, only none of the information she'd been after was related to the Americans. The truth was they weren't important any more. Even if she'd been able to tell them anything, it would have made no difference.

'What you mean is you'll kill me quickly after you and your goons have had their fun with me.'

'It's not the way we operate.' He actually looked pained.

'Yeah, well I don't give a shit about the way you operate but it has to be pretty damn poorly because I don't have a clue what you're talking about.'

Since she was dead anyway, she didn't much care what she said. It was a funny feeling, nothing like any of those portrayed in the vids. She could understand the way people would hang on and do crazy things in the hope they might be released, or find a way to escape. They all hung on too long. It was always, 'Oh, I might have a better chance later and probably he won't kill me'. In certain situations, rare ones, it might have been true, but reality said the choices were a quick death or a slow and painful one.

She was in a building built to withstand a bomb, surrounded by armed guards. She had no chance of escape and therefore no reason to play the game.

'Hacking into one of our military computers.'

She laughed. Not only did it put them off, it really was funny. 'You poor pathetic tweedy little man. Hacking is for losers who don't know what they're doing and mostly can't get it up. They don't even know how to play with yourself, I mean themselves.' The mistake had been deliberate.

'Then why were you in one of our military computers?'

'I wasn't.' Then she realised she had been. 'Oh, the crappy old thing you think is so special.'

'Ah, so you admit it.'

'Admit what, little man? I admit your systems are so crap anyone can get through the firewalls without trying. I was after another tale. I opened the link to where I usually shop for them, put in what I was looking for, something I'd heard about, a new window opened and I was swamped by garbage. Didn't want it, so I closed the window and tried again.'

'You expect me to believe it was what happened?'

She leaned forwards as far as she could. 'You wouldn't believe your mother if she told you she gave birth to you, not even with fifteen witnesses and film of the event.'

'This is serious.'

'Yeah, you need some good techs to help you out. Couldn't be bothered with such crap. Seen some of it anyway. You might call it secret, but almost all of it is posted somewhere on the system. Don't mean nothing, I don't deal with it. Let the conspiracy mob have a go at it.'

'The fact remains you hacked the system. Now it might have been you working alone but we don't believe it is true. You are selling it on. You'll tell us sooner or later.'

'Not when I didn't do it. It's what you do, isn't it? Pick on some poor fool who's fallen into your system because your secure links are almost the same as commercial ones and then you can stand up and say you've stopped someone. Why not take one of your boys with their pea-shooters on the streets and knock off a few people.'

She knew he had been put on the spot. Before he could say anything, there was an interruption and a new suit arrived, waving official papers. No one looked happy.

'Major, I believe you are illegally holding one of our people.'

'One who hacked our system, and we have the right to …'

'You have no rights,' the suit said firmly. 'You took armed men of your own in defiance of the convention and snatched one of our people. If you want her, you have to go through channels, or do I have to bring in my people and have the lot of you deported?'

'Be the end of your career.'

'You'd have to take on my boss.'

He pointed to something on a paper and the American snorted and stood. 'We'll have her back in our hands within the day. If you let her get away, we'll make sure everyone knows.'

'The only thing likely to be known is the fact you have been utter fools,' the suit said. 'Now unlock her, take your chains and get out.'

Within a couple of minutes she was left facing the new man. Kat knew she wasn't free and clear. She had just been given a delay and the man had to want something.

'You needn't think you're out of trouble,' he said.

'Because those stupid fools have a link to a commercial site which goes straight into what they fondly believe are their secrets?'

'Rather more than a store of secrets. The machine was tactical,' he replied. 'The link was probably a way for their people to report in.'

'So you know I've done nothing wrong.'

He gave a smile which told her nothing. 'Unfortunately, in this area intent doesn't matter, only what is done. They will apply to take you back to America and, while the courts will drag their feet and demand assurances concerning a fair trial, you will go.'

'Fair trial!'

'Exactly.' He was on the ball. 'I know you're no hacker, though I have reason to suspect you might be a slider skilled at finding the information some people would rather wasn't known.'

'Then they shouldn't leave it on open access.' She wondered if he had found her lock-up.

'I could agree,' he said, 'and, apart from your unfortunate stumble into the American military system, there is nothing to say you have ever stepped outside of the law. However, it will not carry weight. They will argue you had got into a tactical system and could have given sensitive material to an enemy or messed with their orders. As I say, it is the only thing which interests them.'

'You want something.' It had to be the case.

He nodded. 'I have information which suggests you could be of use to us. We will protect you from the Americans.'

'What's the catch?' she asked.

'The catch, as you put it, is you work for us. You will have to go to work as required and you will have to live where we tell you. You will be tagged and not able to move beyond a defined area. It will give you access to shops and entertainment, with some limitations.'

'I'll be watched all the time?'

'Of course.'

'So you have someone for free to do all your dirty work?'

'Goodness no.' He looked shocked. 'You will be paid at the relevant rate, which, after you have your living expenses deducted, will allow you to live fairly comfortably. It is better you are not seen to be any different from any other young Civil Servant.'

She knew what she was being offered and it would take away her life, or most of it, but she didn't have a lot of life. If she was free, even if limited, she could find ways around any restrictions, at need. She agreed and went with the man.

He took her to a modern apartment block in the centre of London. It was like a barracks, but many singles in London lived the same way. At least it had rooms and she had facilities to do her own washing. Everything from her flat seemed to be in her new home with one exception, and she suspected it was already on its way to America.

'You will have access to all the best equipment and to systems denied others to do the work. Naturally, you will not be able to bring anything home with you and you will not be allowed access to computer equipment away from the office.'

'What do you want me to do?'

'I'll take you to the office along the route you will walk every day.'

The journey wasn't far though all the way cameras were watching her. The office was in one of the big anonymous buildings in Whitehall, so she was close to the centre. It took nearly an hour to get in.

'It will be easier next time,' he told her. 'You have your pass now, though everyone has to be scanned in and out of the building, for security reasons.'

Security was a joke. It always had been and always would be. Once a secret was shared, it was no longer a secret and, with every extra person brought in, it became weaker. They could check she wasn't smuggling bombs into the building or taking files of any kind out. She couldn't swallow a flash drive. It would be seen and it would dissolve in her stomach.

Kat didn't take to Mr. Timpson, the section head. Everyone else studiously ignored her. Her desk, the place she was to work, would be in the corner, furthest from the exit. It contained only a standard terminal.

'You'll have a full set up,' the suit said. 'We always start with the basic links.'

'All about where the line goes.'

'Well, obviously not through the local central processor, it would reveal too much. Shall we?'

They went into the glass cubical off the section head's office and closed the blinds.

'You will have special access and list anything you might need to be passed to me,' the suit told her. She didn't miss the look he gave Timpson. 'Otherwise you will work normal hours and report to Mr. Timpson.'

'Might have a need to do odd hours,' she replied. 'Some things are better done when everyone else is asleep.'

'In time.'

Kat wasn't surprised. She would be on probation and supervised. She worked out Barry Timpson was an administrative suit, not an expert in computing.

Timpson started on the rules but she stopped him. 'I ain't gonna be your standard twonk,' she said. 'I been pushed into this so I'll come and do the job you want me to do. I won't spit or fart, I won't come in pissed and I'll behave myself in my down time though I reckon you think the odd bop wouldn't be right. All the rest I do my way.'

'Within reason,' the man said. 'This is not your chosen profession after all.'

'What do I need to do?' Kat asked.

'If you would, Mr. Timpson.'

Timpson left looking pained and the man ran through what was needed. Basically, there was a big mess at the heart of the British Secret Service machine. It had been checked, double checked, and the designers had been "questioned" because every designer left in back doors in case anything went wrong. They couldn't discover how the machine was being accessed.

'In addition, you might be asked to do a little sliding,' he concluded. 'It will be specialised work. We have our own people to do, shall we say, surveillance tasks. We will need you to look at the people we can't get to. Obviously, checking out people you meet socially will be allowed but no personal work, of course.'

'Yeah, I'm a cog in the machine and you own me body and soul.'

'No, we own your time and what is sometimes laughingly referred to as your loyalty. What you do with your body is mostly up to you as long as it doesn't lead to your arrest or embarrass us, and I have to say drug use is completely out, though I happen to know you don't use. As for your soul, if you could prove it exists, we would be very grateful.'

'Still a prisoner though.'

He nodded. 'Think of it as a suspended sentence or being out on parole.'

'This ain't a security section.'

The man agreed. 'This is Information, the logical place to put you. No one here has your security clearance so you will not pass on all you know. You will give your findings to Mr. Timpson to pass on, but you will not divulge how you reach them or any evidence you uncover which might be needed in taking action. If what you find is someone stumbling on things, accidentally accessing systems or playing the fool, I will leave it to your discretion as to what you say and you can discuss those matters with Mr. Timpson.'

'Get the idea.'

'You will also have a coded means of communication to reach me if you think something is urgent or something serious is being ignored or something minor is being given too much attention. Use it sparingly.'

Her remit, therefore, was to sort out the big mess at the heart of the British Secret Service machine, and find a way out. Kat was under no illusions once she had the main problem dealt with. They wouldn't keep their promise but would throw her right back where she had come from.

Building the trap door and the sand tunnel as insurance were tasks she had already completed. No one had spotted either of them. She hadn't expected them to find anything, because she was the best.

It didn't take long to have her system up and running, it took longer to get it configured to suit herself. The Security Machine, wherever it was located, was state of the art. Once she got into it, she stopped thinking of it as a machine. To her it was Arnold, an upper class twit with a broom handle so far up its arse it could barely move. Barry Timpson was pretty stiff. She always called him by his first name because it annoyed him, but nevertheless he showed some human characteristics. Leastways, he'd noticed she had boobs.

'Where did you get this material?' Timpson was waving the sheets she'd printed off.

'Where the hell do you think?' He could be so stupid. 'Miss Wilson, hacking was what got you into ...'

'Yeah, yeah but it ain't hacking, is it, because you lot had to give me the way in to sort the mess and it's in the mess, floating on the edge of the cesspool, if you like.'

'The cesspool?'

It was as if he was speaking another language, because he couldn't understand her.

To be fair, she was naming things as she went along because she had never, but never, seen anything like it before. So much was in colours and patterns, even pictures which had to be broken down because the pixels had a code which needed to be translated to machine language to make any sort of sense.

'What I calls it because the bloody place is full of shit and pulling in more all the time.'

'Language, Miss Wilson!' He stared at her. 'Whatever is creating the problem is pulling in data?'

'If it's what you calls it. Half of it ain't worth having and most of the rest is out of date. Thing is, it ain't going nowhere and it ain't being eaten. It's bloody crazy. Now let me get on with it if you want an answer before you retire.'

He took her literally, like he did so often. 'You think it will take so long?'

'If you keep bothering me.'

She'd spotted a shape, like a fish, no, a shark. She just managed to grab its tail and then it pulled her into the mess. It was as if she was really there, being sucked down, deeper and deeper into the mass of bits and bites and discharges.

'Miss Wilson!'

She was in the chair, her head back and he was flapping with a folder. At least he hadn't undone any buttons, since if he had probably her boobs would have spilled out.

'Bloody well leave me alone.'

'What are you looking at?' There was a door on the screen. 'I sincerely hope you are not playing games in work time.'

'Pick up, you pointless twitch! This is what's going on. This is why your barmy mates in the land of grey and pink can't find anything. Go and play with your memos.'

He moved away and she opened the door, only to fall down a slope and land with a bang. She was ready for something to happen and simply waited. Not reacting would sometimes work as well as taking action. She was getting the nasty feeling whatever was going on was happening in real time, which meant an operator, or a set of them.

The screen slowly came back together with a simple message.

HEY KAT, KNEW YOU'D GET THIS FAR, WELL REMEMBER IT ACTUALLY. THIS IS THE SPLITTING POINT. YOU GOT ANY SESEN YOU'LL WALK AWAY.

In the bottom of the screen was a small, satisfied looking, black cat. It was her symbol. Someone was playing head games with her, someone who knew her well, and there weren't too many of those.

The message itself didn't make a lot of sense, though whoever was talking to her couldn't spell the word, which was a bit odd. Usually word messages were cryptic, or badly spelled throughout, or perfect. One word wrong was a message in itself and what did it mean about her remembering it? She had never been there before.

A splitting point was easier to understand, basic computer science, the virtual gate where all the answers were every answer. It was a moment when a single action by a single person could make for a colossal change. If she was the person who would make the change, she didn't have a clue what to do.

Walking away wasn't an option, not unless she wanted to spend the next however long it took her to getting to the point of giving up and dying, slouching around in an orange jump suit, when she wasn't having various nasty substances shot up her bum, water poured down her throat so she was continually drowning and being brought back and, for an encore, being used as a sex doll by all the guards.

She took apart the word SESEN. The temptation had been to reply. The machine had been waiting, but she had turned to her second station and worked from there, coming back from behind and dissecting it. Whoever was at the other end missed the first move and then found they were flanked. If she'd gone on looking at her screen, she would have been knocked out.

'Miss Wilson! What are you doing?'

'Solving your bloody problem.'

She guessed whatever was going on at her station was being repeated everywhere else, but her second line wasn't through the main office system. It had been, but she'd made a few alterations.

'Oh, my twisted knockers!'

She was into what appeared to be a live feed from the external cameras, only she knew it was impossible. She could get into them no problem, but the clock on the wall, ancient, running by itself so not likely to be messed with, showed it was mid-morning and what she was seeing had to be late afternoon.

There was something odd about the traffic. It was all the same, pods like in one of the late night programmes. She saw herself exit, not in normal dress, more like Timpson and she was older.

'Miss Wilson, unless you can stop this attack or whatever it is, I am going to activate the master shut down.'

'No!' He was so twitching thick. 'If you do, you'll wipe the whole bloody system, no files, no programmes, nothing. Let me get a handle on it.'

She didn't think she could, but there was a quick glimpse of a location. She saw it was coming from her main terminal, no, it was being reflected from there and it was coming from her base machine. The toy soldiers had taken what they thought was her computer but it was only the one she used at home. They didn't know about her base.

Why was it coming from there?

It was no time to worry or the stupid twitch

Timpson would shut down the whole of the government machine. While it might not be a bad thing in some ways, all the records would go, so no benefit payments, no hospital appointments and so on.

'Gotcha!' She'd set up the system and it was good. She was good. There was no one to touch her.

'What was happening?'

'You ain't got the clearance,' she called, 'but I'm almost there.'

Then it would be time to deal. They might think they could use her and then toss her to the Americans but she had a few shocks for some people. Those pictures of the PM's partner for one thing. The dog looked so surprised. A few more minutes and she looked like the dog. She had an answer.

All she had to do was secure her line of escape. Just because she had seen herself leaving the building in the future didn't mean she had a future. Well it did, but simply one future amongst many and she couldn't be sure it would be the preferred one. She would work it out.

Slime Dog Willy was a complete twitch who thought he was so clever. He had beaten the system, but he had screwed it up big time. She knew how to undo it and she knew when to undo it. His big mistake was he couldn't help but boast, like he'd done something clever.

She also knew who had put in the link which had landed her in a world out of time. It had been Kat Wilson. She knew why she had done it. It had been so she could be right there and sort out SDW.

Of course it wasn't Slime Dog Willy's fault completely. He'd been caught out and put to work for the games players, the people who thought they were so important. He had told them what he could do which, basically, was put one over on everyone, only it wasn't the way the world worked. It was not the machine which was the problem, it was how it was being used, which was true of everything.

'Miss Wilson.' Timpson looked worried, no, haunted. 'This report says I could be a risk to American intelligence due to my posting to Geneva and my links to Arnold, whoever he might be.'

'So?' she asked.

'It's dated five years ahead.'

She nodded. 'Don't worry about it. Might never happen. A lot of random stuff is going on, well it goes on all the time but we never see it. It's just being reported this time.'

'In English, Miss Wilson.'

She looked up at him. He probably wasn't a bad man, though he wasn't really intelligent.

'I found the problem,' she said.

'An attack from a terrorist organisation?'

She nodded. 'Section Seventeen.'

He frowned. 'Computer science?'

'Exactly.' She smiled at him. 'The idiots picked up a hacker known as Slime Dog Willy. Word was he was good, but he put it out using his own Meerkats and he's not half as good as he thinks. They put him together with their people working on the new Quantum Computer and it got out of hand. The mess is happening, because it's processing in all the times which exist, using all the data. We all know what it means when you lot are running your system, load of conflicts. The machine's got a headache.'

'Are you serious?' He shook his head. 'So, we shut it down?'

'Sort of,' she replied. 'First, change the order to pick up Willy. His name's Bertram Howard Smythe, by the way. It won't be made for another forty-seven days. We put in a work order with an 07 code to grab him and he's never allowed near anything delicate.'

'It will fix the problem?'

'If he doesn't work on the machine, make it easier, but it would be better if it was never used. Once it is switched on, odd things will happen.'

'Right, I'll get on it.'

Around the room, the stations were looking normal and the cesspool had vanished, though walls had gone up. Still, she had her sand tunnels and the trapdoor. Kat Wilson was also missing from the system, or rather she was still in it but listed as a consultant to the department. The record which had been tagged to her was tagged to Ping Morgan. It would teach her to grab what Kat had wanted, though he probably hadn't been worth it.

She walked out whistling, free to go where she liked, though it would have to be home. She didn't have anywhere else to go.

Using the information she had found, she suddenly had a lot of other when's to go, which would be interesting, making her the mistress of time, for a while anyway, and she was going to make sure they never caught her out again.

KAREN MCCREEDY has always loved watching and reading science fiction and fantasy, though it was not until she moved from London to the south coast in 2005 that she was able to devote more time to writing.

In 2009, she was runner-up in the "Chichester Observer" Christmas story competition with a sci-fi tale called "Prize Turkeys".

A flash-fiction story, "Payback Time", was published in eBook format by Fiction Brigade in 2012; a longer story, "Chasing the Shadow", appeared in the science fiction anthology RealLies (Zharmae publishing, 2013).

Karen has recently enjoyed some success with supernatural stories, three of which will be appearing in anthologies by Horrified Press. She is also working on her first speculative fiction novel.

BAD MEMORY

[Access Personal Files]. Nothing. As though the Memory Chip isn't there. My chest tightens with anxiety, my breathing shallows to panicked gasps. I remember my name: Steven Koval, I learned that pre-Chip. But... where do I live? What do I like to eat? Who are my friends? Why does my head hurt? Where am I right now - what is this metallic, twelve-sided room, and who are those people crowding together over there by the transparent wall, pointing at something outside?

[Access Information Files]. They work! Relieved, I take a steadying breath, pressing a hand to my chest as my initial alarm abates a little. The Information Chip in my head tells me that the "room" I'm in is one of earth's space-elevator cars.

The crowd over by the window must be admiring the view. I step across to take a look, edging into a gap between an elegant black woman and a bald Hispanic guy in a purple travel suit. In front of us, two small children stand with noses and palms against the reinforced glass, as though smearing themselves against the window will make the view clearer.

The slim blue arc of the planet's atmosphere is visible against an inky sky, the vista below us a palette of colour, shrouded with an ever-changing pattern of swirling white clouds.

It's daylight below us, and from up here even the cities look stunning - sprawling webs of brick and glass thrown down on a varicoloured backcloth. We're too high to see ground traffic or people, though a contrail over the mountains marks the flight-path of an airliner. It all looks so beautiful, so tranquil.

Unfortunately, the children promptly ruin the serenity. 'Wherezit?' shouts one, while the other yells 'Wossat?' Someone murmurs a reply. I don't quite catch what they say, but the words 'calm dow' obviously weren't uttered.

The youngsters continue to squawk and point, while the adults around me sway their heads as they compete for viewing space and confer about exactly which countries we can see from here.

Looking straight out again, rather than down, I realise I can't see the curvature of the horizon as well as I could a few minutes ago. So we must be descending, and heading for [Access Information] London Greenwich. I must have docked at the space-port a short while ago, and now I'm…

Running away.

The words pop into my head from nowhere, and I realise my natural brain function is trying to take over from the malfunctioning Personal Chip. Trouble is, it's not had to store extraneous information since I was five, so I don't know why I'm running, or who - or what - I'm running from.

Like everyone else on earth (and its colonies), I was Chipped when I started school: an Information Chip to store what we learned, and a Personal Chip to store names, addresses, friends, enemies, and everything that went with them.

The Work Chip was added later, another means of clearing the central cortex of information overload and allowing it room to evolve, to grow, to truly *think*. [Access Information]. Since the Chips were perfected, fifty-two years ago, the human race has cured cancer, the common cold, and the mysteries of the universes. We have intergalactic travel, long healthy lives, and - for some - the evolution of new mind skills such as telepathy.

I'm not telepathic, it seems. I don't hear the thoughts of my fellow-passengers, only their voices, shrill and annoying with excitement as they jab their fingers at the view below, pointing out the landmarks and features which are starting to take shape below the swirling clouds. No one seems to know me. No one acknowledges me, or calls, 'Hey, Steve, look at that!' the way my parents did when I was small.

Are my folks still alive? Where are they? I have a sister somewhere too - she was born just before I started school.

Am I married? Have I been married? There's no ring on my finger, but maybe I'm between contracts. Maybe I have children of my own - though, if I do, I hope they're better behaved than the giggling pair of irritants who are shoving each other about in front of me.

[Access Personal Files].

Still nothing, a blank. I search the pockets of my travel suit but all I find is a ten-credit paycard. A quick check of my Information Files tells me that that won't get me very far. But it doesn't really matter: I have no idea where I want to go.

This is frightening, disorienting. I feel a bit queasy. Will I ever get my memories back? Is this file-loss something that can be fixed?

I search my Information Files again, but I've got nothing stored under that heading. I open my mouth to ask if anyone knows anything about this sort of problem - but the words *running away* circle my mind and I think perhaps I should try to work things out by myself.

I move away from the others, tired of their squawking, their garish travel suits and the odour of perfume and sweat. There are upholstered seats around the sides of the car, none of them currently occupied.

I sit down, scratch an itch where the seam of my travel suit rubs against my shoulder, and pull a News scroll from the cylindrical container attached to the armrest. It's a forlorn hope that something on there will help me with my Personal Information, but I'm getting desperate.

I unroll the plastifilm and rub a finger along the soft surface to scroll through the headlines: *Floods in China - Bumper Crop of Blue Wheat - Asteroid Miners strike Platinum - Minister for Extra-Planetary Affairs caught with Martian Settler's Wife.*

I access my Information Chip to compare these headlines with previous examples. As I suspected: different words, same scenarios. There's certainly nothing that strikes any sort of chord with me.

I rub my chin, wondering what I should do when we reach the ground, and discover my face is furry with beard growth. Is this a new look for me? One more thing I can't remember.

We're passing through the clouds now, vapour and raindrops obscuring the view. Everyone takes a seat, save for the two kids who run round in circles, squealing like [Access Information] excited piglets as they chase each other. My head throbs. I glare at them, then glower around to see who they belong to, but everyone else is smiling indulgently. Idiots! Hope the little brats get a Behaviour Control chip when they start school, it would serve them right.

'Anything interesting been happening?'

The voice, so loud, so close to my right ear, startles me. It takes me a moment to realise that the guy in the purple travel suit has sat down next to me, and is pointing at the News scroll I'm still holding.

'Oh. Same old.' I pass him the scroll, hoping he'll shut up and leave me alone. No such luck.

'Been out to the Eagle Nebula,' he confides, mistaking me for someone who cares. 'Checking the sampler drones. My company's got the maintenance contract.' He nods, obviously satisfied that his self-importance has come through loud enough for everyone to hear.

I catch the eye of the elegant black lady as she turns from the window, and she gives me a sympathetic shrug and rolls her eyes. 'What's *your* line of work?' asks Mister Loudmouth, in a tone that suggests nothing I do could possibly be of any value.

[Access Work Files]. They're functioning! Or… are they? I can access the information, but it stops abruptly at a time-stamp several months past. Strange. But at least I now know I have a back-up Personal File at the office. It will be out of date, of course, but better than nothing.

Mister Loudmouth is still waiting for an answer.

'Oh… er… I work in the R&D section at Cobalt Engines,' I tell him, though I've no way of knowing whether that's still true.

He grunts, as unimpressed as I expected him to be, but the elderly woman on my left pipes up. What is it with people in confined spaces that they always feel the need to *say* something?

'Cobalt Engines? Wasn't there something in the news about that a little while back?' she says, her pale pink bio-mechanical eyes blinking as she accesses her Information Files.

Just as she opens her mouth again, one of the screaming kids notices that we've cleared the cloudbase and dashes to window, shouting: 'Look! Look!'; instead of imparting what she knows about Cobalt Engines, Pink-Eyes gives a little 'ooh' of excitement and scuttles off to gawk at the city below.

I try accessing my own Information Files, but I can't find anything on Cobalt beyond out-of-date share prices and press releases. If the company did make the headlines for some reason, it must have been after I went to… wherever it was I just got back from.

There's an attention-seeking 'bing-bong' from a loudspeaker in the ceiling, and the elevator announces we will shortly be arriving at our destination. *'Thank you for travelling with SpaceLift Incorporated,'* it squawks, as though there's a choice. *'Please remember to take all your belongings with you. Welcome to earth.'*

[Access Information]. The Customs desk is at the top of the elevator. I must have been cleared through before my Chip went down. Well, at least I won't have the embarrassment of being stopped at the barrier and led away like a criminal.

The elevator car slows to a stop. As the doors slide silently open, I'm rocked back in my seat by the heat and smells from outside.

Mister Loudmouth chuckles as he activates the anti-gravity floaters on his suitcase and pushes it toward the exit: 'Damn, but I always forget how hot it can get in the summer!'

The little screamers have gone, and old Miss Pink-Eyes follows, her perfume trail almost masking the smell of [Access Information] coolant, polish and people. I look around, but I don't appear to have any luggage. There's not so much as a briefcase left under the seats, and the overhead lockers hang open, awaiting the bags and cases of the upbound passengers.

I hold up a hand to shield my eyes against the glare from the sun as I step out of the elevator. [Access Information]. Mid-afternoon. Mid-August. There'll likely be a storm before dusk but, meanwhile, I need to do something about my watering eyes.

I cross the concrete apron which surrounds the elevator apparatus, and gain the air-conditioned shade of the Spaceport Terminal. Bright lights from holographic advertisements

90

and flashy shop fronts don't help my space-attuned eyes, but there's a small stand in the middle of the concourse selling sunglasses. My Information Files tell me that the prices are outrageous, but I manage to find a pair for less than ten credits and I pay with the card I found in my pocket.

If only I could buy something to shield my ears too - the din is overwhelming. All around me, people are calling and waving, chatting, laughing, crying, and holding loud conversations with distant contacts via their subcutaneous phones. The assault on my ears makes my right temple pulse with pain, and I finger it gingerly. Yes, there's definitely a lump there, a bruise forming. Either I hit my head on something or... *running away...* someone hit me.

I head across polished grey tiles to the main exit. No one shouts 'Steve!' or waves frantically in my direction. If I have a family, they haven't come to meet me - maybe it's an unhappy relationship I'm running from? All the same, I press my right forefinger to the implant in my hairy jaw to see if my own phone is working. Maybe I could call someone...?

Nope. Nothing doing. I didn't expect it to come up with any personal numbers - they're accessed via the broken Chip after all - but the absence of work numbers is worrying.

Either my Work Chip is also damaged, or the numbers have been erased remotely - which would mean I definitely *don't* work for Cobalt Engines any more. Still, it's the only lead I've got, so I get a street plan from my Information Files and board the moving pavement, heading north down the hill towards the Thames.

The air shimmers with heat, the water reflects a cloudless sky, and I'm glad of my travel suit, which senses the temperature and automatically adjusts its inner lining to compensate. Hah! At least I possess *one* piece of technology that works.

The pavement's crammed, and I realise I'm on the travelator which runs from the ancient Royal Observatory.

I'm surrounded by happy tourists, comparing pictures and footage they've taken on their special glasses, while their children tug on their arms, wanting attention.

I catch snatches of conversation -'got your best side...', '...those timepieces...', '...want a wee! ', '...craftsmanship...', '...delete that one...', '...meridian line...', '...I'm *hungry*!'

I'm hungry too, and I wonder when I last ate. As we trundle past the Cutty Sark and on to the bridge over the river, a travel-vendor on [Access Information] a Fastrack board glides through the crowds, slowing now and again to sell someone a pasty or a pie or a cup of tea. He stops his trolley nearby, and I catch the smell of chicken and hot pastry. A glance at the prices on his holo-display tells me I can't afford to eat right now, and I tighten my fingers around the plastic paycard in my pocket. If only I hadn't blown most of its limited credit on the sunglasses...

The pavement branches right and left as we slide on to the northern bank, but I sidestep on to the central travelator which moves straight on through the financial district. We've lost the tourists at last - they're strung out along the embankment, picnicking; or heading for the DLR.

On this section of pavement, there's just me and a scattering of business-types in smart suits. I'm aware that my own travel suit looks out of place, and I make an effort not to stare around me like a tourist. The last thing I need is an interrogation.

At [Access Information] New Canary Wharf, most of the suits get off. Golden buildings, designed to look like stacked coins, throw the streets below into deep, cool shadow.

I take my sunglasses off for a minute to check the street names against the directions on the map I downloaded, then push them back on in a hurry as the pavement clears the corner and the sun slants across the squat dull greys of the Docklands' industrial quarter.

There's a grinding noise beneath my feet, and the pavement judders to an unscheduled halt. The few people who've travelled out this way grumble and curse as they step around metal safety barriers. A hovering repair-bot beeps intermittently as it runs a scan over an open maintenance shaft.

Behind the bot, a hologram points the way to a Temporary Back-up Travelator. I decide not to bother with it as I can see Cobalt Engines up ahead, on the left. A few hundred meters of perambulation along the faux-brick walkway leaves me exhausted - I've obviously not been getting enough exercise - and I pause to catch my breath.

There's a low wall built around the swathe of artificial grass at the front of Cobalt Engines' property. A functional concrete walkway cuts through it to the glass-fronted entrance of what is/was/may be my workplace.

I stand by the wall for a minute or so, staring at the building as though gazing at it will bring my memory back; but I see only a black steel and spun-titanium shell, which bears a superficial resemblance to the casing of a plasma-drive engine - just as my Work Chip recalls. The sign over the door is new to me: "Cobalt-Lockheed" it now reads, in blue, meter-high letters.

Things have indeed changed since I was last here. I guess that must be what old Pink-Eyes was trying to recollect on the space elevator.

I file the new information away in my Work Chip, then head up the driveway to the door. It used to stick as it opened, and make a scraping sound where the bearings were but now, as I take off my sunglasses and stride on in, it glides faultlessly aside on silent runners.

They've refurbished Reception too. The cobalt blue carpet is the way I remember, but the desk has been moved from the left to the middle of the domed space. The company's new name is stretched across a floating banner above the head of the young redhead on Reception. [Access Work Files]. At least she hasn't changed.

'Hi, Angie!'

Her eyes widen in shock, and her intake of breath practically turns the room into a vacuum. 'You! Oh my God!'

I barely have time to register her unexpected reaction before she slaps her hand down on the desk and a klaxon begins to issue deafening two-tone notes which echo around the chromium walls.

Two hefty security guards in full Kevlan body-armour run toward me, stun-guns raised. I drop to the floor as they yell 'hit the deck'. Clearly, my association with Cobalt Engines had not ended well, though I do think the scream and the guns are a bit of an overreaction. When they get out the handcuffs and tell me the police are on their way, I'm astounded.

I try to lighten the mood: 'Hey, come on guys, I've heard of being on the carpet, but this is ridiculous!'

They don't speak; they certainly don't laugh.

They haul me to my feet and push me past the Receptionist who is clutching her neck with slender fingers tipped with blue nail-varnish which matches her official-issue blouse. Her other hand taps the desk again and the klaxon stops. 'I can't believe he'd be stupid enough to come back here!' she says, as though I'm not present.

One of the guards palms the lock on the door behind her, and his buddy shoves me through into the room beyond. [Access Information]. It's the sort of functional space security types have occupied down the ages - a table in a corner with ladder-backed chairs each side, tea-making paraphernalia on a shelf, a creased poster for a five-year-old netgame on the wall over the table, screens feeding information from cameras around the building, and an all-pervading smell of stale food.

Playing cards are scattered across the carpet. One of the guards picks them up, dumps them on the table and pulls a chair into the middle of the room. 'Siddown.' His voice has a menacing edge that suggests argument would be a bad idea.

Bewildered, I lower myself on to the worn upholstery, trying to get comfortable on the lumpy seat. My shoulder itches again, but this time I can't scratch.

'I don't understand,' I say. 'My PC has gone down. I don't even know where I live, let alone what I did wrong. What in space is this all about?'

The guards - cloned from the largest, meanest stock in the vaults - raise identical eyebrows and fold identical muscle-bound arms. They stare down at me, then look at each other.

'Scanner?' says the one on my left, the one who wielded the handcuffs.

The other nods. 'Scanner.'

A moment later, he produces a handheld [Access Information] Chip Reader and passes it back and forward over my right temple, just where my head hurts.

'Nuffink,' he grunts. 'It's dead all right.'

'Like the Prof,' says Cuffs. 'Serves him right.'

'The Prof?' I access my Work files and find a match. 'You mean Professor Baxter? Doug? His Chip went down too?'

I hear Scanner-boy put the Chip Reader on the shelf behind me. He circles around, leans in close enough for me to recoil from his onion breath, and snarls: 'No, you Chipless idiot, his

Chip ain't dead. He is. And you know what, Memory Man? You're the one what killed him!'

'What?' I access my Work files again, searching for an answer that isn't there. I can find only mutual research work and a regular diary appointment for lunch with him at the *Rocket and Handcart* every Thursday. 'There must be some mistake.'

'There isn't.' The new speaker stands in the doorway, flanked by two MetPol constables. He wears a SpacePol travel suit which looks almost as battered as his face - his handsome Eurasian features are smothered in blue MediGel, his right eye partially closed by a fist-sized bruise. He holds up a holographic badge. 'Lieutenant Conlin, Space PD.'

Cuffs waves a hand at me. 'He's all yours, Lieutenant. His PC's fried though. He won't be able to tell you nuffink.'

Conlin strolls toward me, thumbs hooked in his stun-gun belt. 'Not a problem. There was plenty of time for him to 'fess up while I was bringing him back from Orianis Three.'

He looks at me, taps his head. 'All above board - recorded in my Work Chip, and backed up on the ship's computer.' His mouth twists with annoyance as he addresses the security guards. 'He was making such a good job of co-operating, I let my guard down once we'd cleared Customs. Told me he needed a comfort break before we entered the elevator, then whacked me when we got to the Gents. I whacked him back - guess that must have taken out his PC - but the bastard used my own damn gun on me. Next thing I remember is waking up on a cold wet floor with the cleaner shaking my arm. We'd just started up the Locator Grid when your alarm call came through.'

I shake my head, trying to take in the enormity of it. I'm still getting to grips with Doug's death. Being asked to believe I killed him is too much to take in. 'I don't understand. I only recall Doug as a colleague, a drinking buddy. He was a nice guy - maybe a touch on the arrogant side over his research, but who isn't? What possible reason would I have to kill him?'

Conlin moves a few paces forward to stand in front of me, and folds his arms. 'Doug Baxter was a latent telepath. He'd been going to evening classes to try to boost his ability. Do you remember that?'

I sigh. 'Which part of "my PC isn't working" don't you get? If Doug told me any of that, I'd have filed it under "personal". It had nothing to do with work, and it's not the sort of information I'd have much use for.'

'You sure didn't have any use for it when he managed to read your mind.' Conlin taps a finger against his temple, then points it at me. 'It would only have been hints, flashes - he wasn't adept enough to get more than that before you stored the experience in your Chip, but it was enough. You and his wife.'

He makes a "tut-tut" noise and wags the finger. 'Naughty! Anyway, the poor sod confronted you, there was an argument...'

The finger stops wagging and Conlin draws it across his throat. 'Lights out for Doug Baxter. You hoped his wife was fond enough of you to give you an alibi, but she called the cops and you ran.'

I'm pulled to my feet by the MetPol guys, too stunned by all these revelations to offer even a token resistance. 'I don't remember Doug having a wife,' I mumble. 'I've no recollection of her.'

'Then you won't miss her when you're sent to the Uranium Mines with only a Behaviour Control Chip to your name,' says Conlin.

The two MetPol guys frog-march me toward the exit. 'Maybe there's something to be said for a bad Memory after all.'

PRIZE TURKEYS

'Skipper, we have a problem.'

The voice on the shuttle-pod's communications speaker sounded resigned rather than panicked. Which indicated that at least the Spacefreighter they were making for was not in imminent danger of blowing up - but it didn't make for much of a welcome either. Especially not when you were the Captain of the freighter in question and you were heading back to your vessel after two weeks' leave.

Isobel Pritchard sat up straighter in the co-pilot's seat, and looked across at the pilot. 'Did my Chief Engineer just say...'

The pilot, an old acquaintance who had made the journey into orbit with her many times, looked as puzzled as Pritchard felt, but merely nodded in response to her question.

Pritchard sighed. She had had a relaxing holiday in Hawaii, and spent a week catching up with friends and family, safe in the knowledge that the SpaceDock crew were more than capable of loading the freighter in her absence. She had been looking out of the shuttle-pod window, trying to see the lights of other merchant spaceships, when the message came in.

Leaning forward, she thumbed the communications control. 'Chief, this is Pritchard. What sort of problem can you possibly have in SpaceDock that can't wait till I'm on board?'

'Ah.' She heard the engineer clearing his throat, and pictured him pulling on his grey-flecked beard as he always did in times of crisis. 'Well, the problem just now, Skip, is… um… we can't land the shuttle-pod in the hangar. You'll have to dock at the emergency air-lock. Sorry.'

'Hangar doors still playing up?' Pritchard was annoyed. Chief Engineer Conlin always insisted on remaining on board during layovers to make sure he could deal with such difficulties while he had access to SpaceDock facilities. It wasn't like him to have let something so basic get by him.

There was that throat-clearing noise again. Pritchard wondered whether she should just turn around and go home for Christmas while the technicians sorted out whatever the problem was. Then Conlin spoke: 'The doors are fine, sir. It's just that the hangar's already full. Of… turkeys.'

Pritchard saw her own bafflement reflected in the pilot's expression. 'He did say "turkeys", right?'

'Uh-huh.' The pilot checked their course and keyed the controls to make a minor adjustment, while Pritchard thumbed the comms switch once again.

'Chief, we ordered half-a-dozen oven-ready turkeys for the crew's Christmas lunch next week,' she said. 'Please tell me how this constitutes a hangar-full?'

The sigh at the other end of the comms channel was the type which usually heralded news of an engine burnout. 'This is something you really need to see for yourself, Skip. I think there's been a mix-up somewhere.'

'Oh, not again!' Pritchard remembered last year's fiasco all too vividly. They had forgotten to specify "oven ready" on the order form and, when the crates had been opened, six live turkeys hopped out and chased each other round the galley. There'd been gobbling, feathers, and mess everywhere but, once the creatures had been recaptured, none of the crew had had the heart to dispose of them. The birds had been shipped off to a sanctuary, and the crew had dined on reconstituted pork - garnished with a sprig of fake holly to add a festive touch.

Echoing Conlin's sigh, Pritchard shook her head and said: 'OK, Chief. We'll be with you in three minutes, and will dock at the emergency air-lock per your advice. Pritchard out.' As she offed the switch, she added: 'I should never have left Hawaii.'

It wasn't far from the air-lock to the hangar deck, but Pritchard metaphorically fired all thrusters as she barrelled through the narrow corridors. The deck's shipside access hatch slid open, and she started her tirade even before she stepped through it: 'All right, Chief, this had better be...' She halted mid-step and mid-sentence.

In front of her, six film-wrapped turkeys occupied the floor. Each one was labelled "Oven-ready". Each one was approximately the same size as the shuttle pod she had just left.

As Pritchard stared, the ship's cook climbed out of the neck of the nearest bird and descended a ladder that had been propped up against the gullet. He was muttering something about 'stuffing', and Pritchard's thoughts echoed the sentiment.

Heavy footsteps on the decking heralded the arrival of Chief Engineer Conlin. The burly Irishman had a hand on the Quartermaster's shoulder as he propelled the smaller man in front of him. The engineer wore the expression of a policeman who had caught some villain in the act. 'Welcome back, Skip,' he said.

'Thanks, Chief. I wish I could say it was good to be here.' Pritchard jerked a thumb at the turkeys and addressed the Quartermaster. 'Cruz, care to explain this... this... insanity?'

Cruz ran a hand through his black curls and gave an apologetic shake of his head. 'I'm sorry, Captain. When these things arrived, I dug out the original order. Got a printout here somewhere...' He patted his pockets, located a creased sheet of paper and handed it to her. He jabbed a slim finger toward the upper right corner of the form. 'Here's the problem. This should read "Montana", right here.'

Pritchard studied the type he was pointing at. 'It says "Monsanta",' she said and, as Cruz nodded, went on: 'So it's a typo. How did that get us... these things?' She waved the paper at the turkeys as she spoke.

Cruz folded his arms and sighed. 'I've tracked back the order,' he explained. 'It seems it was misdirected to a low-gravity farm on New Monsanto.'

'The genetic engineering planet?'

'Yes, sir. Apparently we are the first lucky recipients of their experimental "two-ton" turkeys.'

'Yippee.' Pritchard's tone was darker than the interstellar void. She glared from Cruz to Conlin. 'Did we *have* to take delivery? I mean, isn't there a get-out clause in the small print somewhere?'

Cruz nodded. 'There is. But the penalty payments are heftier than the turkeys. We figured we'd better just bring them on board, and sort out the details later.'

'Details!' Pritchard snorted, folded the form and handed it back to Cruz. 'Half-a-dozen oven-ready turkeys - how difficult can it be? Last year, live birds, this year...' She took a breath.

No point losing her temper. It was done and, after all, Christmas was coming.

Which gave her an idea.

'Cruz, there are lots of ships and freighters out there which haven't had the opportunity yet to stock up for Christmas.' She remembered the number of space vessels she'd seen from the shuttle-pod. 'Let's give them the chance to take part in a great seasonal tradition.'

'Captain?' Cruz looked baffled, the Chief Engineer quizzical.

'A raffle, Mr. Cruz,' said Pritchard, 'And, if you make back the money we've spent on these things, you might even have a happy Christmas yourself.'

She smiled across at Conlin, and gave a last glance at the turkeys. 'Clear the hangar deck and depressurise, Chief. We've got turkeys to refrigerate.'

THE BAD QUEEN

I knew from an early age that the entire kingdom revolved around Me. True, I didn't have the best start in life, daddy having been eaten by a dragon shortly before I was born, but mummy always made it clear that I was a Very Special Little Girl.

'Do get out of the way!' she would call to anyone who had the temerity to walk on the pathways I drove along in my toy carriage. 'The dogs will have your ankles if you don't move!'

I knew that was silly. Fang and Bruiser were sweet hounds, who loved nothing better than to pull my little carriage over hill and dale for hours on end; they wouldn't really bite anyone. But oh! what fun it was to tug on their reins and aim them at somebody's legs. Knocked a little girl in a red cloak clean over one day, near the edge of the woods, and everything spilled out of her basket. I did laugh!

On the rare occasions when we had to take the horse-drawn coach west to visit my wicked old grandma, mummy made sure I had a seat, even if it meant other folk having to travel on the roof. 'I'm so sorry,' she'd say, 'but I think my little one is coming down with a cold. You don't mind sitting outside, do you?'

No one ever objected, though that might have been because mummy always tapped her wand against the coach window frame as she spoke. She never actually *threatened* anyone - even the peasants could take a hint. I was always a bit disappointed when they climbed up next to the luggage without a word of complaint.

Those journeys could have been really boring because there wasn't ever anything to do except sit and look out of the window; but a little squealing, wriggling about, and kicking anything within reach always brought out the pacifiers: gingerbread men, a magic flute, chocolate biscuits...

It wasn't long before I learned that if we went out anywhere, I only had to *hint* at a tantrum and mummy would rush to indulge my latest whim: sweets, treats, toys, new dresses, sweet-smelling perfume, sparkly tiaras. She never said 'no' - at least, she never said it more than once. That's how I got my first wand for my third birthday - yes, yes, I know many would say that's far too young, but I wouldn't be Queen today without so much early Magic practice.

Naturally, it helped that I was gifted, but mummy was such a darling. She taught me every spell she knew, paid for extra wizarding tuition, and gave me everything I asked for. Well, almost everything. We did have a teensy squabble last month over her wonderful magic mirror. The one the palace footmen are just hanging on the wall in my new dressing-room.

Dear mummy. Now our little quarrel has been resolved, I like to keep her nearby as a reminder of my humble beginnings. There she is, look, by the side of the pond. Third toad from the left. You can tell by the white stripe on her head where her hair used to be. I'll pop out later, and tell her all about the wedding.

It went well, I think. The King was handsome and elegant in a high-collared blue velvet, while his little Princess looked suitably ordinary in the drab cotton dress I'd designed for her. She was so thrilled to be a bridesmaid, I don't think she noticed her shoes squeaking or cared that the petticoat was cheap and scratchy.

Her father thought it was a lovely gesture on my part, asking his little girl to share our Big Day. But I was only doing what was necessary to keep him under my spell.

I've always done what's necessary, mummy will tell you that - if you speak toad.

I must have been about five when I managed to cast my first proper spell. Mummy had found a governess for me, a horrible woman who had the gall to suggest I should tidy away my own toys, pick up my coat instead of dropping it on the floor, and use words like 'please' and 'thank you'. I practised my toad spell on her and, although it didn't quite work as it should, I was thrilled that I'd managed to make her catch flies with her tongue, smell of the swamp, and say 'ribbit'.

Mummy magicked her back to normal, and told me I would get on much better in life if I learned my Ps and Qs, but my governess left the next morning. I saw her from my bedroom window, floating over the trees beneath her open umbrella, and made a note to learn how to throw lightning - it would have been such fun to have dropped her into the woods, smouldering.

Mummy said she should have been cross with me, but seemed more amused than angry. 'You must learn your reading and arithmetic, darling,' she said. 'How else will you be able to read your spell-books and be able to calculate accurate doses of potions and poisons?'

Well, since she'd put it that way, I did try to be more tolerant of the next governess. And the next. And the one after that. Problem was, they were all far less talented than Me. Gradually, I learned a concoction here and a spell there, and began to understand when it was prudent to feign politeness. Take the King, for example, (and I have) - even with my strongest magic, I'd not have been able to bind his heart quite so well if I hadn't kept up the pretence of good manners.

I'd climbed up the social ladder, of course, by the time I met him. Mummy used a spell or two of her own to get Me presented at court, and she used the last of daddy's Life Insurance to make sure I had the best rooms and the latest fashions.

'Weave your friendship spells on the jousting crowd, darling,' she said, 'and the unicorn-riders. Don't waste your time with anyone who isn't heir to a title. You're worth nothing less.'

Poor dear Podge. Such an easy catch mainly, of course, because no one else wanted him, with his extra blubber, his stammer and his terrible dress-sense. So grateful for a little attention from Me that I didn't even have to bother with the love spell.

True, he was only the second son when I met him, but it wasn't long before he became heir to the Dukedom. *Such* a shame about his older brother - unicorns are usually such passive beasts, aren't they? I wonder what caused it to turn on him in that way?

They certainly were an accident-prone family. The Duke fell off his own battlements; Podge's sister pricked her finger on a spindle and is still in a coma all these years later; the Dowager Duchess banged her head, lost her memory, and wandered off to live in a gingerbread hut in the middle of the forest.

It was fortunate that we had so many good friends at the palace - they were all *so* sympathetic. 'Poor Podge, is there anything we can do?' they asked, and the answer was, of course, invitations. Lots and lots of invitations, to palace parties - dinners - jousts - dances - receptions. Any function the King might attend, any event where he might notice Me and realise I was the fairest woman in the land.

The Queen was pretty enough, I suppose, in that vacuous way blondes have, but she looked terribly *delicate*. The first time I set eyes on her, I said to Podge, 'She doesn't look strong, that girl,' – and, sure enough, within the month, she was lying-in-state.

'Poor King,' I said to the courtiers. 'Is there anything we can do?'

I must admit that a year of court mourning rather strained my patience, but I amused myself by casting little spells on Podge. The constant (and rather embarrassing) itch was comical to watch, and I had hours of fun when I turned his reflection into a donkey.

By the time I got tired of the jokes, and persuaded him that he needed to confront the troll under the bridge who had undoubtedly put a curse on him, the palace was back to normal and the invitations had started to arrive again.

'It's what he would have wanted,' I assured everyone, as I bravely attended my first court dinner without the Duke. Magnificent in purple, I accepted the condolences with a brief inclination of my head, and a faintly-quivering lip.

'My dear Duchess,' said the King, as his jewelled fingers touched mine, 'how I empathise with your loss. Is there anything I can do?'

You know the rest. A brief courtship, a tiny binding spell, a sumptuous wedding in the cathedral, and here I am - Queen of all I survey.

The footmen have finished adjusting the mirror. Doesn't it look wonderful with the light gleaming off that gilded frame, and the velvet curtains draped on either side of it? I shall stand in front of it and admire my new crown, then ask it to remind Me how beautiful I am.

The fairest of them all.

For ever.

ANNE OLERENSHAW. After a variety of mini careers and lesser jobs at home and abroad, Anne studied, as a mature student, to qualify as an English teacher. Most of the rest of her working life was spent in Further Education, teaching English and Liberal Studies.

Her writing reflects this eclectic trend by exploring various themes. She prefers writing plays but also enjoys working on short stories in different genres: humour, horror, fantasy, romance and more.

As a happily retired and pensioned person, Anne now feels free to write whatever she wishes, within the bounds of decency and the law, without having to fear the trials and tribulations of starving in a garret.

THE REBIRTH DAY PRESENT

I may be immortal but I'm not infallible. Even so, I've been delegated to record events as they happen. The others say I'll be the least likely to leave anything out. I think they just see me as a soft touch and a bit pedantic.

'Anyway, it's your turn,' they remind me. 'Do your best.'

As it happens, I don't need to go back to the very beginning, even if I could; we get only occasional recollections of how things were before - a sort of timeless state of bliss, like being submerged in a translucent amber lake.

Whenever we emerge, something we call Time begins again, which we chop up into manageable portions. We have to invent things to do, and to find ways of getting on with each other - extremely trying after a long and peaceful slumber.

At first, we creep about, taking care not to make a noise or do anything irritating or speak out of turn. In short, we readjust to a new state of being; to re-learn the trick of living as individual entities in four dimensions.

Eventually, though, having once more come to terms with our condition, we set about organising existence in ways calculated to satisfy our needs until the next Elysian submersion. We devise games and entertainments (I've been advised not to go into detail about those!); hold competitions for beauty or athleticism and create new works of music and sculpture.

Each of us aims to surprise and delight the others with something new until we weary of it all. You see, we need none of it; for us, dreaming it is just as meaningful as doing it, but that takes up none of the time and space which hangs heavily upon us in our changed state.

Then, as this record began, the one known as Dunno made an interesting suggestion. He said, 'Every time we materialise, we become distinct from each other and of different ages. Maybe we can think of a special way of using this circumstance.'

After debating the matter, we decided it would be diverting if we were each to choose a personal name and a portion of time which might pass for a birthday, or a rebirth day. Of course, we have no calendars, nor any seasons, either, but we did manage to invent names for the periods of time ahead of us, as far as we could make sense of such an idea.

The one who called herself Lili, incarnated as a matronly lady, showed some foresight in this. We'd just completed the choice of rebirth days when she pointed out: 'As my rebirth day comes first, I must be first to get the party and the presents.'

A bit of resentment flared before a general agreement - after all, what did it matter? Joe, a disgruntled-looking fellow, recently out of his teens, was the only dissenter.

'It's not fair,' he whined. 'By my calculations, I'll be last.'

'But think about it,' Aurore tried to appease him, 'you'll benefit from our experience of giving presents and throwing parties. As yours will be last, we'll make it the best, a grand finale with fireworks and the kind of surprises only we can devise.'

Joe was mollified by these words and consented to wait his turn.

I won't go into the myriad wonders of these events but with our special powers we were able to produce some marvellous effects.

For a while, we managed to pass the time happily enough. Nearly everyone expressed satisfaction with their rebirth day surprises but, as Joe's day approached, we wondered what we could give him that would surpass the others. He had waited so long and expected so much. We couldn't disappoint him, especially as he had helped devise great parties for everyone else, although normally he was rather peevish and demanding, in my opinion.

It was Panda who finally outlined an original idea for Joe's present. Mind you, it wasn't going to be easy and it took maximum effort from everyone to get it ready for the occasion. Even then, we weren't sure it would work or how acceptable it would be. It didn't look very impressive as we gave it to Joe on his rebirth day.

'What is it?' he demanded, adding none too politely, 'it looks like a load of grit.'

'What did you say?' asked Lili, sharply. She was a little hard of hearing.

'"Grit",' said Alun, helpfully, before turning to Joe. 'Whatever it looks like, it's made from a special formula as befits a special person's rebirth day.' Alun could be a great flatterer. 'And it comes with magic potential, as we know how much you enjoy experimenting.'

'Well, what am I supposed to do with it?' came the truculent response.

'It's a kind of Do-it-Yourself Kit,' suggested Panda.

Joe's frown deepened.

'More like a game, really,' I said quickly, knowing that games and practical jokes were Joe's favourite occupations. 'Where's the rest of it?' I asked the others. I meant the components, our individual contributions. We hoped the parts would work well together as planned, but there hadn't been time for a dry run.

Buddy took it upon himself to explain: 'Look, this is just the starter kit. Once assembled and activated, all kinds of interesting things happen because of the inbuilt randomness. It means that every time you play with it, you'll get different effects. It's unique. No one else has anything like it.'

Joe was not easily convinced. After his initial sulks, he became absorbed in the new toy. We couldn't help looking on to see how well it was functioning which was probably a mistake because most of us got hooked while Joe, noting our interest, started getting above himself and bragging about his expertise. We might have considered taking him in hand, except that he was leaving us behind fairly quickly. But at least his preoccupation meant he wasn't being quite as obnoxious as usual.

Before long, the game had begun to engross everyone. Instead of the expected aeons of boredom, we found ourselves avidly watching as aspects of the game constantly reconfigured.

Occasionally, we were allowed to make suggestions, which Joe would use if the humour took him. But he was also secretive, doing things behind our backs. The next time we looked, the game had moved on and we had a job to keep up.

You see, as we had cobbled the kit together, we had no clear picture of its true potential. Our guidelines for its use recommended the creation of beautiful kaleidoscopic patterns, but Joe had his own ideas. In his impetuous way he had tossed the 'grit' around like confetti, which I considered a most ungracious way to treat our gift. As the bits scattered, they joined up to form bigger pieces which collided like rocks, creating spectacular incandescent effects which we all enjoyed.

Later, Joe made the rocks dance to his tune, some dizzyingly fast, others ponderously slow, while even more were fizzing and exploding like fireworks with magnificent flares of light, or spinning away with tails flying in a great cosmic wind.

Joe soon tired of the pyrotechnics and concentrated on a few of the smoother rocks which took his interest. He set about making special blueprints for what he said would be a remarkable project. We looked on, fascinated. Before long we saw a result. One of the rocks was changing colour.

'What's happening?' we asked.

Joe rudely tapped his nose.

'I know,' said Aurore. 'It's sprouting a park, something like ours, though not quite so pretty. But what are those?' She pointed to a number of strange, animated objects, either crawling on the hard surface, moving about in liquid, or being airborne, trying to escape from the rock.

'All my own invention,' boasted Joe. 'And I haven't finished yet.'

Well, of course we knew our input had been key, but we had left gaps and loopholes in the set-up, little guessing how Joe would choose to fill them.

At that stage, when we could admire the beauty and ingenuity of the toy, we felt flushed with success. We had managed to capture Joe's whole attention, while creating an entertainment for everyone else.

'I hope you're recording all this,' said Lili to me.

'Every last detail,' I replied.

One day, we found Joe unusually absorbed as he played with his game. He had somehow managed to invent a couple of artefacts which looked and acted suspiciously like himself.

'Are you sure this is wise?' asked Dunno.

Joe twitched nervously. 'It wasn't me,' he claimed. 'It just happened. It must be the way you designed the thing. I always suspected there was something wrong.'

'It could turn out interesting,' suggested Panda. 'What harm can there be in it?'

I dare say most of us were thinking that anything looking or behaving like Joe would benefit from careful supervision, at the very least.

Joe pre-empted us. 'I'm taking no chances,' he stated. 'I'm going into the game to take a closer look at those creatures, or whatever they are, to make sure there's no mischief-making.'

We found this decision worrying but could offer no rational opposition as Joe assumed a stern front and merged with his game. He returned, looking smug.

'They'd already gone too far,' he asserted, 'but I've had words with them and sent them packing. They won't find their conditions so easy in the future.'

We were slow to understand, but it was obvious that Joe wasn't telling us everything. Had we confiscated his toy at the first hint of trouble, it wouldn't have come to this.

Caught as we were between fascination and consternation, we let things slide as the situation went from bad to worse. The creatures had clearly become self-willed.

Before we could act decisively, the little reprobates, far from being chastened, increased their numbers. They were cocking a snook at Joe and everyone else, behaving in ways which were shocking, even by our standards.

None of us had actually resorted to murder, as they had. Nor did it stop there. Having got the taste for blood, they engaged in such carnage and general destructiveness that we thought Joe's toy would be ruined.

Alun was appalled. 'This can't go on, Joe,' he began. 'If those things are part of the game, you should be able to control them. What are you going to do about it?'

'I'll tell you what I'm going to do,' Joe replied. 'I'm going to drown the lot of them!'

'Isn't that a bit hasty?' I asked. 'After all, it's not entirely their fault.'

Buddy pleaded with him. 'Give them another chance,' he begged. 'They'll learn, given time.'

Joe thought for a moment, moved by the strength of feeling.

'All right, a final chance, then - a fresh start for one deserving pair of each design. But if they won't do as I say, it's curtains.'

It was a sad period as we watched the inevitable consequences of the rising tides. Joe, true to his word, saved enough of the creatures to start again on a firmer footing, or so we imagined. But before long they were up to their old tricks, and in even larger numbers.

'Look at that!' cried Dunno, suddenly. He was pointing to a tall structure which was aimed menacingly in our direction and growing by the minute. 'It's a threat, I'm sure.'

'Don't worry,' Joe said. 'I'm dealing with it.'

I don't know what he did, but the whole edifice started to crumble.

'They won't try that again,' he asserted triumphantly. It was the only solution, of course. By now, I'd developed an admiration for the little devils. Yet as time went on, Joe became more agitated.

One day he called us to a meeting.

'Any suggestions,' he began, 'before I throw in the towel?'

'Maybe you're too hard on them,' offered Buddy. 'Try being nice.'

Joe glared at him. 'You try,' he sneered. 'I don't think they understand "nice".'

'Perhaps we're worrying too much,' I suggested. 'At least they've helped to relieve our boredom. The naughtier they get, the funnier they are to watch and they can't hurt us.' A few of the game watchers agreed with me.

Alun raised his voice. 'And let's be fair,' he said. 'Many of them bend over backwards to please us.'

Only to curry favour,' sniffed Joe, taking the cynical view as usual.

'What about those gatherings they have, to say agreeable things about us?' Dunno asked.

'That's just flattery, empty words,' claimed Joe.

Panda spoke. 'Face it, Joe, you're a control freak. Why don't you just loosen up?'

Joe was furious. 'It's my toy and if I can't control it, I don't want it! I've tried talking reasonably to these creatures; I've entertained them with magic and stories, I've given them simple rules to follow, I've chided, threatened, punished and nearly destroyed them, yet they are determined to go their own way, come hell or high water.'

I interposed. 'It may be your toy, Joe, but every one of us has had a hand in it one way or another. We're as interested in its fate as you

124

are. Why don't you take a little rest from it while we see what we can do. No promises, mind. If you're not satisfied, we can always scrap it and start again. What do you say?'

'Get on with it, then,' he replied. 'Let me know when there's a result.'

The truth is we didn't really want to scrap the toy; our current existence had been greatly enhanced by its invention. Our best bet was to adjust it to within acceptable limits.

I was to play a large part in the next stage of the game. I became personally involved by interacting with a number of the artefacts. It was a creepy experience, I can tell you. Some were pleasant enough; others extremely nasty.

When I appointed fellow creatures who could act as their representatives, many were set upon and killed - including one of my favourites. But, to give them their due, he was remembered with respect.

Eventually, we devised methods of gaining enough control to satisfy Joe. When many of these didn't work, we hatched a foolproof plot. We led them to believe that at the end of their time, we could assign them a new existence in one of two places: one filled with pleasure, the other with torment. Their eternal fate would be at our discretion, depending on their current behaviour. It was surely a simple choice and it should have worked.

However, it was not a brilliant success. Most of the creatures didn't believe us, some who believed didn't care and the rest just paid lip service to the idea. I don't think they grasped it. Much of the time they were too busy making use of the resources built into the game. They had developed a will to survive, and an inventiveness to rival our own.

At first, we took the credit for their cleverness, until we found that their stones had become arrows, then blades, then bombs, with worse in prospect.

We could only wonder at, and even envy, further innovations. Before long they could create any conceivable object, even new versions of themselves by methods we had certainly not sanctioned. Could they ever discover the secret of immortality and become our rivals? What had gone wrong?

Joe had his accusations ready: 'Look what you've done! Don't say I didn't warn you. I'll show you how to handle this bunch of delinquents.'

He grabbed the controls and was about to switch them off when something strange happened. Joe disappeared. I mean he vanished, like an extinguished light. Before we had time to panic, Panda also faded out. One moment she was there; the next, nothing.

'Perhaps we're due back in the amber,' said Lili, complacently. 'I'm looking forward to a rest until the next little episode.'

'But we usually go together,' I reminded her, just before Lili dissolved.

At this point, the rest of us looked at each other wonderingly, until the silence was broken by a distant amplified voice. We had no choice but to listen in amazement as words from one of the creatures assailed us.

'Hear and take note, Losers,' it began. We gasped at the insult, but the voice went on. 'We're at the end of our patience. When we created you, you took an interest in us and often did our bidding, though we found you arrogant and temperamental. We overlooked this because we had bigger problems to solve. We've reached the point where we no longer need you. As once you helped us, now you are hindering us, even daring to threaten us, so we've decided to boot you back into limbo, probably forever, and that's a kindness compared with what you deserve. If you bother us again, we'll repeat the penalty. Do you understand?'

We were weak with outrage but Aurore marshalled her strength. 'We made *you* - you are our creatures, part of a game,' she declared.

They responded with raucous laughter.

'It's true,' said Alun. 'You're nothing but a bagful of animated dust.'

'Which you claim to have propagated?' asked a mocking voice. 'Mumbo jumbo. You're all freaks and monsters. Some of you are gone already and the rest of you have only moments left, so prepare yourselves.'

I've no idea how long the creatures had been plotting this mutiny. How could they have done it without arousing suspicion? How could they have done it at all? They're just bits and pieces of a game, I reminded myself, as I awaited further revelations

I have continued to tell the story, until this moment, when there is only silence and my own thoughts. I look around and find myself alone.

My hand is shaking as I express my fears. Why have I been left until last? Of course. I'm being given time to finish the work I started. Then what? I'm thinking of my erstwhile companions, wondering if they have become as one again in the amber bliss and if I shall soon join them.

Something tells me this is the end for all of us. And even as I try to hold on, I can feel myself passing into oblivion. I hear another, gentler, faint voice from the spinning rock.

'Don't go,' it's saying, in a pleading tone. 'Some of us believe we got it wrong and we're truly sorry. Please forgive us and we'll try to do better. If you go, we must go too. Imagine what we might accomplish together, if only …'

128

The voice is fading. I'm mortified and sad, but also helpless. The creatures have clearly not realised the deadly force of their own powers until now. Nor had we understood our own limitations.

I know I'm almost done for but I'm making the effort to finish my task: 'It's too late,' I'm trying to say. 'Too late ...'

J S ROGERS has degrees in psychology and education, and former careers in advertising and university teaching.

She reads voraciously and eclectically, and writes short stories, mostly speculative fiction and historical/althistory. Her short and flash fiction has been published and short-listed in competitions across these genres.

Having lived on four continents, she has now settled in the west of England. When not writing, J S Rogers gardens, teaches, eats and drinks in local tea shops and pubs, as well as walking the Somerset Levels and surrounding hills with her husband.

CALYPSO SOLO

Calypso Mission Log: Landing Day +3
Log recorded by Psych Officer/Biologist
Emily Harris

Crash landing on Calypso. Cause: lateral engine failure. Dead on impact: Mission Commander Jenkins, Science Officer Wu and Medical Officer Buczynski.

Engineering Officer Adams and I were thrown clear. Dave has broken ribs and a bad leg injury. I have a deepish but clean cut to the right thigh, now stitched and healing; no other injuries.

The dead crew were buried with curtailed rites, as Dave needs constant attention. Burial ground is north of the Hab site, makeshift grave markers in place.

Have commenced Hab assembly, slow work on my own. Damaged lander is providing shelter for now.

Oxygen/nitrogen mix is close to Earth normal, and though air temperature is low, dipping at night, I have used GrowZone insulation to maintain the lander environment to barely adequate.

+10
Hab complete; salvageable kit transferred from lander. Hydroponic GrowZone oriented to

south of the Hab. Water production online. The soil here is dry, colours more to the red/blue part of the spectrum than on Earth. When dry, shades of lavender and pink predominate, when wet it's almost purple. The air is so dry at this season on Calypso, in the mornings I can see clear across the plain to the surrounding hills, colour of bruised plums.

Dave is in sick bay. Mostly dozing, has been speaking in confused snatches. Now unconscious; high fever; red raw puffy skin round his compound leg fracture. Giving him antibiotic shots, but he really needs major surgery.

I'm no surgeon!

+26

Dave died today. Am now alone on this uninhabited Earth analogue, twenty-four light years from home.

Our mission ansible was amongst the kit destroyed in the crash, so instantaneous communication with Earth is no longer possible.

I'm uploading log reports to the orbiter as a mission record for historical purposes. Maybe someone will find them useful if a second mission is ever sent to Calypso.

Took stitches out of thigh a few days ago; skin warm, a little swollen, normal healing.

Seeds in the GrowZone sprouting. Should be able to transfer seedlings to the outside farm area, and produce a harvest well before the rations run out. Air temperature still cold, but the soil is warming.

+46

Spent the long Calypso day out in the rover. Landing site is on a broad plain, bleak at this season and ringed from south-east to west by the red hills we imaged from orbit. Craggy, impassable by rover; no further exploration possible.

On the plus side, found two water sources below a dry creek which runs from hills south past Hab.

Temperatures currently range between minus five overnight to plus fifteen daytime. Accumulating climate data indicates that overall days are lengthening and warming. Diurnal variations of light wavelength are interesting: dawns are green-tinted, ranging through bright pink by noon and shading off to bronze at sunset.

+57

Feeling low. Spent some time at Dave's grave, on the sunny side of the Hab by the farm. Think I wanted him near for company.

As the mission Psych Officer, I understand the human need for company. Found myself wittering on, telling him about the Hab, the crops, the logs sent to Mission Control. Not sure he'd think the logs a worthwhile effort.

+60

Being a biologist is proving useful. Analysis of local Calypso soil is encouraging: the necessary range of nutrients and acceptable level of microbe activity. Soil temperature and sunlight now sufficient for seedlings to be transplanted to the farm.

Have set up irrigation channels from the nearer water hole, hoping for rain or snowmelt. Till then will rely on water production from the Hab support unit. Told Dave the good news on my visit to his grave.

+65

AM. Good long rain last night. Creek bed running a stream, irrigation channels brimming. Spent the morning planting out seedlings in polytunnels: maize, peas, tomatoes to add to my rations.
PM. Surprised on checking the seedlings to find the maize has already sprouted new leaves and multiple stalks. Not normal growth for maize, but no complaints if I get a bigger crop. Maybe responding to Calypso conditions? Growth metre confirms they've shot up six to eight centimetres since yesterday.

+66

AM. Problem: power supply stopped during the night. Apart from plunging Hab temperature below zero, means overspill heating to polytunnels isn't functioning. Seedlings will die tonight if I can't fix the problem.

I'm no IT expert: that was Dave's area.

Wearing my torn spacesuit for warmth this morning, checked solar panels and batteries. No issues there.

Eventually found that software managing the climate controls had crashed, but couldn't trace the fault. Kept hearing a silly saying of Dave's, 'Try turning it off and back on.' God, I wish he were here, solving the problem with his strong capable hands. Suddenly feel so helpless.

PM. Thinking of Dave brought up the mental image of that bit of kit he used to fix everything. He called it a 'sonic screwdriver' - some kind of old joke, I think. The mission inventory calls it a "solid state reboot interface". I can auto-start the system with that. No sign of the tool in the Hab or lander, though. Only one place it could be: in his overalls.

Evening. Steeled myself to exhume my friend. So sorry, Dave. Dreaded uncovering him, but dreaded equally not locating the screwdriver. I found his overalls and the screwdriver all right. Then I dropped the spade, scrambled out of the long shallow pit in horror. Couldn't think or breathe.

No body. Not even bones. He's gone.

+67

OK, work the problem, came a thought. Didn't seem to be my thought: a man's voice, Dave's, pushed into my mind. I sampled the soil round the grave. Nothing obviously abnormal. A lot of fibrous root systems, but this area is close to the maize field.

Retching, I dug out the north burial site. Found three bodies - the remainder of the crew, right where they should be, and how they should be after nine weeks of decomposition. Filled the graves, forced myself to walk steadily back to the Hab, where I fixed the climate control OK. Thank goodness for the sonic screwdriver.

+68

Couldn't sleep. Calypso has always felt empty, but safe nonetheless. Now it feels threatening. Either I'm mad, or something weird is going on. Solitude causing hallucinations? The psych evaluations I run weekly say I'm sane, whatever that means.

How can the law of entropy apply to the rest of the dead crew, but not to Dave? Makes no sense. What is different about Dave?

Eventually I slept. And dreamt. Dave sitting next to me, his face turned to mine but not in conversation. And yet I seemed to hear: *You're not mad, Emily. Use your training. Keep working the problem.*

Waking, for an instant I saw Dave's shape: bulky, strong, energetic.

Spent the day out in the rover. Bare plain round the Hab now transformed - covered with varied plant growth, mostly clumped shrubs with leaves all colours from violet to pale green. Only three weeks after the previous trip; phenomenal growth!

Took soil samples and specimen cuttings. Thick sticky sap extruded and then coagulated from each specimen. Really gooey. Stuck to my skin where glove was torn.

+72

Analysed my samples. Repeated the tests three times - same result each time. All living organisms on Calypso have identical DNA, a long complex sequence. Soil shows the same extensive networked roots I found in Dave's empty grave.

Rushed to the farm on a sudden thought to sample my crops. Guess what? The maize plants, peas, tomatoes - all Terran - now show the Calypso genome. But phenotype is still three distinct plant types, recognisably what I planted.

+73

Told Dave about the DNA analyses today. It helps to mull over the weirdness, talking to no one. Today, I was too excited to feel scared: tomorrow I harvest my first crop of peas. Can't wait to have real food!

+74

Dreamt again. Saw Dave fleetingly, indistinct. I thought I heard: *Just respect the living. You'll get what you need.* No idea what that means. Respect myself, maybe; certainly isn't anyone else here to respect. Not even Dave, no matter how much I wish the empty grave means he's alive.

Am I creating illusions? If I find signs of psychosis, what then?

I decide to keep uploading this log.

+75

Peas are delicious! Ate the first few raw, straight from the pod. So ripe they'd fallen off the plant, quite tidily. Then made a tasty soup with chunks of ham-flavoured protein. Next week tomatoes will be ready. Then, oh joy, the maize.

Sun is getting hotter every day. Came back to the Hab with a headache, hard to shake off. Must wear a hat tomorrow.

+81

Dream: Dave's voice telling me: *You will find what you need. Look again.* I can't see him anywhere, just a shimmer from the angled light of Calypso's sun. His voice rises from all directions.

I awoke bemused, worried that my dreams are getting delusional. What is it that my subconscious - manifest in the Dave dream-figure - thinks I need? Ran another psych eval - still normal.

+82

Collected the ripe tomatoes. A pile was already gathered, heaped under the plants. No need for my pruning knife. Odd. Must be an evolutionary explanation. Did Calypso plants evolve to drop fruit when ripe to enhance prompt germination without birds? I'll run some controlled trials next season. If I stay sane.

+85

Woke feeling slightly feverish. Too much sun, despite the hat. Maize corns were waiting for me in an orderly pile on the soil this morning. Second pea harvest will start in a few days, hmm...

+88

Peas in pods, piled on the ground. No avoiding the conclusion. Although I'm apparently the only living ambulatory creature on this planet, someone or something is harvesting my crops for me.

+89

On a whim, checked the plant and soil specimens which have been culturing since collection. Surprised to notice a microbe with different DNA. Not enough to ID as yet. Will check in a couple more days.

+90

Came round from a sudden blackout this morning to find myself shivering and sweating, collapsed in the maize field after a dizzy spell. Crawled back to Hab. Temperature way off the scale. Injected antibiotics, took blood specimen with shaking hands.

+91

Last laugh is on me. I'm ill, but not with a Calypso bug. Somehow we brought a microbe from Earth, maybe in the water system. Can hardly move, headache, hacking cough, high fever.

+92

Antibiotics not working. I'm coughing blood, chest on fire. Can't crawl out of bunk even to pee. Got water by my bunk, but haven't eaten in days. So tired.

+94

Struggling to breathe. Coughing up blood frequently now. These notes from brief lucid intervals between coma-like sleep. Hallucinations, too.

Saw Dave outlined in the Hab door which I must have left open when I staggered in three days ago. Couldn't make out his face, but heard his voice, low and husky. *It's too late now, Emily. We're out of time.*

He faded into piercing light. I found myself twisting in sweaty sheets, then floating up, away from the pain and heat, giving up the desperate struggle to breathe.

+95

Woke suddenly, in the dark. The agony in my chest had gone, and I was back in my own mind. I felt cool, dry, clean even. The Hab door was shut, but I could see from my bunk a small light at the workstation, flashing a "report complete" alert from the blood culture analysis. I got up, checked the culture results. Legionnaire's Disease. I should be dead.

I looked again at the Calypso samples of plant material and soil. There was my Terran bug again, outnumbered by antibodies swarming all over it. On an impulse, took a fresh blood sample from my arm. Smeared a drop on a slide, under the microscope. A battlefield: macrophages swiftly engulfed the Legionnaire bacteria and wiped them out.

I wasn't going to die after all.

I had a sudden flashback, the image of Dave silhouetted against the light as he leaned toward me from the Hab doorway.

+98

Back to pottering around the farm, but my illness has made me forgetful. Several times I've come to from a daydream, not knowing how I'd got where I was. Taken more blood samples to check for...who knows? Must be something to indicate what's wrong.

+99

Dreamt again last night. Dave, of course. I woke hearing his words, annoyed at the lack of meaning: *It's chemistry, Emily. They never had an interaction. That's the difference.*

What difference? Who's "they"? There is no sign of any intelligent life, or even animal life, on Calypso. No one here but me. And three dead colleagues, who never even....

Oh God, they never took a breath of Calypso air - they died in the sealed lander. They never encountered Calypso biochemistry.

Dave did. He lived and breathed on Calypso for weeks. And so have I.

Back to the lab desk, again. A closer scrutiny of the Calypso genome, now fully sequenced. Some base sequences look familiar, I've seen them before. On the floor near Dave's sickbay bunk, I find what I need. A hair. I add another. A crossmatch will give me results in the morning.

+100
Final Calypso Mission Log entry

The difference is there, in the genes: mine, Dave's, all Calypso life. We're somehow bound together, in a Gaia-type single organism. If future Earth missions arrive here, I'll leave it to them to fully investigate how it happened. I just know Dave has helped me join in a new form of shared life.

I'm at home, no longer alone. Outside the Hab, Dave is waiting for me in the bright Calypso light.

Emily Harris, Calypso Mission Psych Officer/Biologist, signing off.

Final Calypso Mission Log

ANTONY SHAW is a teacher of mathematics, a musician, a reasonably skilled artist and an avid reader of fiction and non-fiction.

A few years ago he wrote, produced and directed several (no budget) short films. He also produced musical videos for the academy where he works.

Since then he has written several short stories and is currently in the early stages of writing a novella. He has five children.

CHARLIE LITTLEJOHN

Unit Number: CLJ10998.
Model: Spherical Cycloptic Robot.
Function: Maintain factory processes.
Capture and detain intruding species.

Much of the factory is shut down for the holiday month of Libuary. Some machines and automated processes are still operational, but most are out of action.

Cyclobots never have time off, and Charlie Littlejohn is no exception. He is on his midnight round and has stopped at a run-down insect store. On a wall, a dim LED counter displays the store's insect count: 0-3-2. He extends a thin, wiry arm and punches the wall, releasing a cloud of dust - the display brightens.

The dust has contaminated his eye: he removes it for cleaning, leaving behind a large dark hole in his spherical body. The eye's translucence partly reveals its internal circuitry - tiny blue LEDs twinkle - rendering the iris a sparkly blue. He polishes it with well-rehearsed dexterity, like a bird grooming its life-saving feathers.

The hum of fluttering wings is picked up by five audio sensors fitted around his perimeter. He quickly reinstalls his eye, then spots an insect up ahead. Reaching for his stun-gun, he takes aim and shoots. The insect falls. He approaches the intruder, pausing to observe its intricate design. He lifts it carefully. It fills his hand. He takes it with him, in an on-board insect-flask.

As he continues his round, he passes a decommissioning chamber. On a wall are signs:

'Few Cyclobots have survived a drop!'
'Maintain your eye habitually -
It all ends here for those who can't see!'

'A loose wire or a blown fuse?
Repair it now or Salvobot pursues!'

He arrives at another insect-store. In the wall, by its entrance, is a small portal. He opens it, placing the insect-flask inside. He retracts his hand, the door automatically closes. Through a small window, Charlie observes the interior of the portal. A mechanical hand lowers and opens the flask. From jets in the walls, a gas fills the portal; winged insects crawl out of the flask. As the mist clears, their wings buzz - separating light in gentle hues and tones.

A shutter shoots down, closing the viewing window; the flask is returned to Charlie.

Progressing through the complex, he pulls up to enter code into a wall-pad; a nearby door lifts. He moves into a large chamber and arrives at the edge of a dark circular expanse. The deep hum of distant power generators is occasionally interspersed by the sound of an object landing somewhere up ahead - in the dark.

Charlie's Central Processing Unit (CPU) instructs him to check the chamber. He presses a large button on the wall next to the door. A clunk is followed by the sound of a motor.

A narrow viewing platform extends slowly over the chasm. Amber LEDs twinkle to life along its edges, giving detail to the space. A large domed roof spans a circular sea of green eyes. Suspended from the dome are several eye-taps: green eyes randomly fall from the taps, plummeting to the sea.

The platform stops near the centre.

Charlie moves along the platform; he spots a cluster of insects circling up ahead. He takes aim. He is about to shoot but, as they head towards him, he fixes on their flight pattern. They fly around him - he turns with them - they spin like whirling litter trapped in a wind.

Two blasts ring out. Two insects fall. A third blast. A third falls. The remainder disappear.

He collects two insects and places them in the flask. The third insect wriggles violently on the platform. He approaches it and, from his utility chamber, takes a small gas-gun - he sprays the insect with gas. Its wings flap - they buzz. It is soon airborne, flying erratically, dazed. The insect alights on Charlie's eye, gathers bearings, then flies away. Sticky deposits from the insect's feet have contaminated the eye - his vision is impaired.

He removes the eye and begins to clean it, but the sticky deposits stubbornly refuse to move. He rubs harder and faster. His CPU over-rides for a status check.

He drops the eye! It bounces rapidly along the platform. Reaching for it, he grabs only empty space; using both platform edges as guides, he takes chase. The eye's decreasing bounce gives way to a fast roll. Over the edge it tumbles.

'Few Cyclobots have survived a drop!'

He extends both arms down to the sea of green eyes below. He lifts the first eye that he touches and inserts it. Green. Black! He hurls it.

Reaching again, he tries a second. Green. Black! He throws it.

He pulls two at a time. Each green, each fitted - each rejected; many bounce several times on the platform, before rolling back to the sea.

He slows - slower - and stops.

CONTROL ROOM.

Salvobot.

Unit Number: SAR300001.

Model: Salvage Robot.

Function: Retrieve and decommission faulty systems.

148

Salvobot data received from mainframe:

Unit CLJ10998 visually disabled.

Action: retrieve unit for immediate replacement - decommission imminent.

Stepper motors whine in staccato rhythm as the Salvobot unit runs through routine motion checks. Tiny white LEDs twinkle along its limbs: checking bus-systems, connections and nodes. Software updates from Mainframe flow into its ports.

Charlie Littlejohn is on the edge. His audio sensors pick up something in the building - in the distance - on the move.

The Salvobot moves swiftly - ploughing its way through the dark factory.

It arrives at the eye-chamber and enters.

Salvobot CPU update:

CLJ10998 up ahead.

Salvobot steps on to the platform then swiftly moves to the cyclobot's coordinate - but no Charlie. The head spins a full three hundred and sixty degrees - scanning the panorama of green. A distant blue glow streaks across its vision.

Mainframe issues a status update request.

Salvobot reports:

Visible contact negative.

Mainframe computes a response.

Charlie hangs with extended arms which span the width of the platform. His hands grip both edges. Above him, Salvobot turns and heads back to the entrance.

Charlie's audio sensors pick up the fall of an eye - his CPU maps its path through space - he waits. It lands somewhere in the sea.

The platform starts to move back in. Salvobot! One hand remains gripped while Charlie lassoes the other over the platform and grabs the opposite edge. He clambers up.

Audio data streams in: CPU maps the fall of another eye. Reaching out, several metres into the dark, he catches it and inserts it.

Black.

He darts off the platform, guessing a direction for the exit door, and makes a run for it.

He is seized! In the struggle, the eye falls from his socket and rolls to the door. He crashes out.

Salvobot drags him out of the chamber; punches the wall-pad. The door drops. They disappear into the dark.

Muffled sounds trickle into his CPU. Audio sensors recover slowly. He begins to recognise some sound. With both hands, he feels his surroundings. Scrap!

A giant metal claw moves along a gantry. It stops. Swings. Drops. Shrapnel flies. Close to him, a large chunk of scrap is torn loose and lifted. It moves along the gantry, disappearing through an opening, into a shredding chamber.

The scrap falls on to a slow moving conveyor belt. At its far end, teeth-like cutters await the unusable, ready to tear it to spaghetti.

Charlie's sensors detect the sound of the claw returning. He pulls the insect-flask from its chamber and opens it. The claw stops above him. He reaches inside the flask. A crash splits the air; a fresh chunk of scrap is grabbed. His feet are tangled. He moves up with the scrap. At height, the claw stops and jerks forward, swinging Charlie violently. It heads for the opening. His hands are empty - the flask falls.

A final green eye drops.

A pause.

Under-floor gears grind as a large prime mover picks up speed. A deep bass rumbles, increasing in pitch as it gathers energy. The sea of eyes begin to jitter, gently at first, then more violently - the sea boils.

At its centre, the eyes move around a circular path. As they pick up speed, they induce others to rotate with them, moving the rotation out, until the whole sea spins around a black hole.

A blue eye circles.

Charlie filters the sound of the fall to his CPU. He reaches down and catches the flask. As he lifts it towards him, his other hand grabs the gas-gun. He releases a small squirt of gas into the flask - two insects fly out and hover around him. He waves them away.

A laser blast skims past. Sparks fly as it hits an air vent in the wall. Smoke clears to reveal a small glowing hole. Salvobot adjusts his aim.

Charlie frantically waves the insects away. Another blast and the flask is hit; it shoots away - spinning through space - taking Charlie's hand with it.

The insects are gone.

Outside in the corridor, smoke delicately rises from the air vent. Two insects appear. They turn right, then head down the passage. Banking their way through the complex, they arrive at the eye-store and hover outside its lowered door.

The blue eye circles close to the hole, its speed increasing as it swirls closer. It disappears into the abyss.

The insects shoot down. In a synchronised dive, they enter the hole. A few remaining eyes continue to circle. The chamber, almost empty, reveals its inverted conical form.

A fountain of green eyes jet violently from the hole, launched by a determined punch. A blue eye shoots through.

At the top of their climb, the insects turn the eye and begin to descend. They pick up speed, wings blur. At maximum velocity they curve, rollercoaster-like, towards the door.

At the door's base, a single green eye has prevented it from fully closing.

Blue light shoots under the door.

Pinned down by the junk, Charlie approaches the metal teeth feet first. His hand-less arm lies immobile, bare wire exposed.

He filters all audio input to CPU, allowing only insect patterns through. The buzz of approaching insect wings filters in. He computes their flight path; they circle overhead.

Two laser blasts ring out, then several more in quick succession. Both insects have taken a hit. They tumble through space. The eye falls.

Charlie's feet jiggle rapidly as he nears the gnashing blades.

Salvobot approaches the conveyor at high speed, pushing aside all obstacles in his path. Charlie's CPU instructs:

Catch eye.

He extends his hand and positions it for the catch. Blades shred his feet, vibrating him violently.

Salvobot is there! He watches as Charlie makes the catch.

The shredding stops. All processes shut down.

Salvobot stands next to the still jaws. A stationary conveyor belt lies before him. Like a lawman who has cleaned up the town, he looks proudly over the scene. Charlie is motionless. In his outstretched hand, two insects lie.

Salvobot presses closed an emergency stop button: his other hand safely clutches Charlie's twinkling blue eye.

In a small workshop inside the factory, there resides a semi-retired cyclobot. His new friend has recently fitted him with a new hand and a pair of all-terrain feet.

He spends most of his time outdoors, in the nearby woods, enjoying the sunsets and the sounds of the world. Some days he suspects he is being followed, or watched. Gentle wings hum in the distance behind him. Rainbow colours flicker and dart between the trees.

His favourite days are these.

PAUL SHERMAN is a teacher, author and director of Youth Theatre in the UK. His stories have been published in various hard copy magazines but, most recently, he has had three fantasy-horror stories ("The Jokers of Sarzuz", "Daemon Page" and "Missed!") published by TWB Press. Shortly to be published is his novella, "Satans Grip".

He has also written poetry and plays which have been performed at various locations in the UK. "The Arsehole at the End of the Universe" (a modern take on the mediaeval morality play "Everyman") was performed at the Traverse Theatre, Edinburgh.

Paul is currently working on a collection of short stories, "Tales out of Herm", which are set at different locations on Herm Island, one of the smaller Channel Islands; his play "Kilmainham Kids", set in Kilmainham Gaol in Dublin, Ireland, has been accepted by Stagescripts Ltd.

VOYAGE OF THE
LOVE DUST CATALYST

Eddie had been gone for twenty-four hours. His parting gift had been the little pot of love-dust in the drawer. Imogen had not yet touched it.

The telescreens relentlessly showed the departure of the fleet – six sleek silver container ships. Imogen had no idea which one Eddie was on. It would be a full earth year before he returned to E.F.I.S-1.

'Use it when you're really missing me,' Eddie had said as they lay in each other's arms. 'It'll help.'

She was missing him already. A dull hole ached in the centre of her body and she moved around the quarters as if in a dream.

She missed his conversation, the little asides, the smell of him - just being aware of his presence. How would she cope?

Even when he was there, it was hard enough to deal with the regimentation of satellite living – the dry air, artificial gravitation, square-screen view of the world, earth thousands of light years away, people she knew (she couldn't call them friends) being overly jolly because life was 'perfect'. Eddie was gone for a year. Life was anything but perfect.

She went to the cabinet and opened the drawer. The small white pot with the simple screw-lid lay there. No markings of identity.

Nothing to say that the powder within the container was the same powder the fleet was carrying by the tonne into the depths of space.

The telescreen burst into the newsman's metallic voice-over: '*Alfred Kreisler, chemist, the man behind beta-PXC9, watched the fleet's departure from Earth Foundation Interplanetary Satellite Control Centre. Professor Kreisler will remain in contact with the mother-ship "Casa Nova" throughout the mission.*'

Imogen picked up the small white pot.

'*Firing operations will be under the control of Professor Kreisler,*' the voice-over continued. '*He intends that the 'love-dust', as beta-PXC9 is popularly called, will have maximum effect on the inhabitants of Gallipoli, Ypres and Verdun, the so-called "problem planets".*'

She unscrewed the lid. It looked innocuous and was, according to Eddie, harmless. A plain white crystalline solid that could be any household substance – in a time and place where households still existed and where the telescreen was not on automatically and continuously.

Yet Imogen was oblivious to the voice of the newscaster.

'It's so easy to take, honey,' she remembered Eddie saying. 'It absorbs through the skin, but to get it into the bloodstream quickly you either sniff it up your nostril or place it under your tongue. When it reaches your brain, you will feel love, honey, just love. And you will think of me.'

'Gallipoleans, Yprians and Verdunians have so far posed no threat to the interests of the Earth Council itself. Recently, intelligence has suggested that disturbing disagreements between interplanetary administrations and warring factions from Ypres, in particular, seem intent upon initiating hostilities against their neighbours...'

A few grains, that's all it takes. In this miniscule container, there was enough love-dust to keep her going until well after Eddie had returned. Yet she hesitated...

'Last week, the Council Commander stated that such hostilities were unthinkable, given the awesome power of their weapons. If E.F.I.S-1 did not become directly involved, its mineral planets nearby would be under severe threat. Indeed, the Earth's economy depends upon them.'

The screen cut to the opulent heavy features of the Commander.

'This is not a situation which we can tolerate,' he drawled. *'We cannot allow our three mineral planets to be subjected to destruction or any kind of contamination at the hands of the Gallipoleans, Yprians and*

158

Verdunians. Earth Command has instructed "Casa Nova" and the fleet to use love-dust to its full potential.'

Imogen had seen archive film of primitive races imbibing archaic drugs through the nose. The idea did not appeal to her. Likewise, to put it under her tongue seemed so invasive somehow. Perhaps she should just rub it lightly into her wrists and wait for it to work, even if it took a little longer.

'Imogen?'

The icy voice startled her so much that she dropped the container into the open drawer. She hadn't replaced the lid properly and much of the crystalline material had spilt. She turned guiltily.

'Abigail!' she exclaimed.

'Are you alright?' Abigail was dressed for duty in her orange suit which had the Information Department logo slashed across the front. Her black hair was tied back efficiently into a bun.

Clockwork Abigail, with the cruel eyes!

'I'm missing Eddie!' Imogen fumbled the drawer closed.

'One of the hazards of dual relationships,' Abigail commented dismissively. 'Anyway, we're on duty. You're not even ready. You're not dressed. You look terrible. What are we going to do with you?'

Abigail went on duty. Imogen promised to be there within minutes. She scooped the spilt powder back into the tub and replaced the lid. The little she missed lay scattered on the notepad. Unhesitatingly, she moistened her finger with saliva, picked up a couple of grains and placed them under her tongue.

Within seconds, she was in Eddie's warm embrace, with fantasies of love obliterating everything else.

Imogen turned up for duty in the Information Section, forty-five minutes late, mumbling apologies to the Section Head who didn't seem unduly bothered. She glanced at Abigail, who did. Sighing, Imogen sat at her workstation and logged in for the shift brief.

'We don't have Kreisler human enough in the reports,' read the rationale. *'He may be a chemical genius, but we need him as a family man.'*

Little was known about Albert Kreisler, the man who believed that human behaviour and emotion could be chemically controlled. There were those who maintained he did not exist, a mere individual identity representing the Earth Foundation Chemical Empire. There was no shortage of film and photograph of him, however - but not apparently, with his family.

'Please produce ASAP a family picture of Kreisler,' ran the directive.

No problem, thought Imogen, and set to work, scanning the picfile.

Photographs of the "chemical genius" abounded in various sizes, coloured and monochrome, some with him smiling, most not. Separately, she found pictures of women and children, homely surroundings, rich warm family environments.

They made Imogen want to cry, but Abigail was looking at her and she didn't want her emotion to leak.

It didn't take long for Imogen to invent Kreisler's "family": a pretty wife with brunette hair, three children (blonde twin girls and a small sandy haired boy). They stood in a spacious oak lounge, in front of a roaring log fire. For good measure, Imogen added an Airedale terrier to the picture. It was easy, as it was the kind of situation she envisaged for herself. She worked quickly and produced another picture to her own specifications; one that was just for her, to look at when she was missing Eddie.

'Don't you realise what's going on out there?' Abigail asked as she spooned her way indelicately through her shift-break meal.

'Mmmm?' Imogen prodded her food absent-mindedly.

'Oh, Imogen, you haven't even been listening! How can you appreciate the import if you don't listen and comprehend? Don't you realise why Eddie's been taken away from you? What he's doing?'

'This whole political thing bores me. I just want him back.' She felt the left hand breast pocket of her suit for reassurance that her picture was still there. She heard it crumple.

Abigail's eyes narrowed, in her usual lizard-like mannerism.

The telescreen crackled and performed. The bulletins were carrying Imogen's pictures of Kreisler and his "family".

'My friends,' Kreisler announced, *'I want to tell you about the importance of this mission.'* His face creased into a smile. *'Without revealing any official secrets, of course.'*

It was talking. The picture Imogen had created this morning was talking. Kreisler's mouth was opening and closing, his wife and children were smiling and looking at him. Even the Airedale terrier got up and changed its position during his speech.

'If this mission is successful,' Kreisler continued, *'then war will never break out between Gallipoli, Ypres and Verdun. Our mineral planets will be safe, and Earth Foundation Interplanetary Satellite-One can prosper and grow. In six months, the fleet will have reached its destination. We must all have patience 'til then.'*

162

Static ensued, followed by the announcement - '*Personal messages. Personal messages. Please return to your workstations.*'

'Come on,' Abigail said. 'This is what you've been waiting for, isn't it?' There was no kindness in her encouragement.

'*Hello, honey.*' Eddie's face and voice came to her, transmitted from deep space. '*Sure am missing you. I hope you're missing me a little too. You needn't be though. Did you use the little present I left you? Don't fret, hon. When I get back from this, we'll go to Earth. Maybe for good. Settle down in that place with the log fire? Well, got to go now, honey. Back to work. Grafting away for good old E.F.I.S-1, eh?*'

The picture faded and died, momentarily leaving a ghost image in its wake. Imogen stared at the screen for ages. Felt her left breast pocket. Stared at the screen. Knew what she wanted to do.

She lay semi-conscious on the recliner in her living-quarters, the picture clutched in her hand, the pot of love-dust on the table beside her. She had sniffed it and the effect was amazing.

Eddie was with her, they had made love, they had talked about earth, they had made plans. Eddie was out in space, yet she could generate him at any time from her little white pot. How the dust enabled her to love him. How it could bring him quickly back to her. She was unaware of the telescreen and Kreisler.

'Beta-PXC9 is a complicated enzyme which acts in that part of the brain capable of causing aggression. It blocks those chemical reactions that lead to aggressive behaviour, enabling all those processes leading to affection, love and forbearance to dominate. Scientifically speaking, it screens the active sites of those "aggressive" biochemicals. In certain concentrations, folks...' Kreisler's attempt at humour, *'...it can even act as an aphrodisiac. But don't rush to your local suppliers. Beta-PXC9 is a strictly controlled substance and is not available on the open market.'*

Eddie moved against her. Imogen moaned.

Nearly six earth months passed. For the last three days, the telescreen had maintained a discreet silence concerning the love-dust mission. Buzz on E.F.I.S-1 had it that the time was approaching. Love dust missiles were being fired. The moment was critical. If Gallipoli, Ypres and Verdun suspected they were being fired at, they would retaliate with their own rockets which would carry dust of a different kind.

Kreisler's re-assuring face had appeared on the screen keeping 'folks at home' in possession of the facts - at least those facts Command Security wanted the 'folks at home' to know.

164

Eddie's last personal message had been the day before the screen blackout.

'*Hi, hon,*' he said. '*Sure am missing you. I hope you're still missing me. But don't fret, hon. Remember what I said. When I get back from this, we'll go back to Earth. Maybe for good. Settle down in that place with the log fire? Well, got to go now, honey. Think of me, often.*'

The message was no comfort, too much like the rest. They might have been mass-produced. With a mild shock, Imogen realised they probably were.

An operator in her department, albeit in one of the inner sanctums, had engineered 'messages home' in the same way that she, Imogen, had engineered Kreisler's home and family. They weren't even done subtly; she was capable of creating a much better fabrication.

'To tell you the truth,' Imogen said to Abigail later that day, 'I find those messages irritating. I'm not sure I'll bother to access them anymore. Especially if they aren't Eddie's.'

Abigail gave a self-satisfied smirk.

'Eddie is beginning to irritate me as well,' Imogen added. 'When I hear him speaking those trite words, I think it's just as well he's on a screen. If he was here in person, I'd slap him.'

She watched Abigail's eyes narrow. She looked more reptilian by the day.

'Slap Eddie?' she echoed. 'Is this the Imogen of the famous Earth-style monogamous partnership talking to me? Is this the Imogen who longs for life in a cabin with a log fire?'

Imogen wondered how Abigail knew about her wanting a log fire.

Security Command came for Imogen that evening.

She had just snorted a liberal quantity of love-dust and was lying on the recliner, awaiting Eddie's arrival. The telescreen was jubilant. Kreisler was in fine fettle.

'The delivery of the product went according to plan. The fleet have spread love-dust amongst the planets. In a few weeks E.F.I.S-1 will contact those "not-so-problematic" planets...' he grinned. (His grin reminded Imogen of Eddie's grin; they might have been engineered by the same operator), *'...with a long-term peace treaty, which we feel sure the Gallips, the Yips and the Verdis will be pleased to accept. In the meantime, our boys have turned round and are on their way home. To wives, sweethearts and mothers out there, we are on countdown to reunion.'*

The apartment door slid open and the love-dust-imbued Eddie joined Imogen on the recliner. He placed his hand on her cheek, then pressed her hands and kissed her. Something was different; it didn't feel the same. She didn't find his touch ... satisfying.

She pushed him away. He faded from view. She closed her eyes, her heart beating impossibly hard.

'Incredible scenes from the planet Gallipoli are being received by "Casa Nova". We are able to bring you these images from deep space."

Eddie returned, insistent, trying to seduce her. On the screen, hard-skinned amphibian Gallipoleans were out of the water, on land, gathering flowers.

Kreisler's voice was ecstatic: *'They're marching on Government House, strewing flowers along the way. Outside Government House, they're gathering in their thousands, chanting peace slogans in their guttural language. Reports are coming in of a colossal love-in on Ypres, taking place spontaneously, in the open air. There is no news yet from Verdun.'*

Imogen twisted and writhed on her bunk, trying to force the ephemeral Eddie away from her. Her eyes were tightly closed and her fists hammered thin air. When she opened her eyes, Eddie had gone. Abigail was there, trying to prevent Imogen's hands from hitting her.

'Sshh, Imogen, calm yourself, it's alright.'

Gradually, Abigail came into focus. She spoke into the radio transmitter fixed to her shoulder. 'Violent initially, but calming now. You can come in.'

The doors of the living-quarters silently opened. Two uniformed men entered, their faces hidden by the characteristic dark helmets of Command Security.

'I have the residual beta-PXC9.' Abigail spoke softly into the transmitter. 'Yes, there's easily enough left for analysis.' She turned her gaze on Imogen. 'This isn't what you think.'

'How do you know what I think?' Imogen was scornful. 'You knew I was using the love-dust, you've known for ages, and you've betrayed me. I always knew you would. Something about your eyes, Abigail. Something inhuman.'

'Flatterer!' smiled Abigail. 'As I said, this isn't what you think. Not at all what you think. It's observation, not punishment. Take her. Make her comfortable. Sedate her.'

Accompanied by Command Security, Imogen left the apartment. Abigail followed.

The telescreen continued chattering to the empty apartment. *The news from Verdun is equally excellent. The Verdunians have, of their own volition, offered the hand of peace to their neighbours. Delegates have been invited to a peace conference to discuss ways in which the three planets can go forward together.*

Solitary confinement reinforced the feelings Imogen already possessed before her 'arrest' by the two men from Command Security. She was well cared for and regularly fed.

The quarters were as comfortable as her own, rather less spacious and a little plainer but there was no element or feeling of imprisonment. There was, naturally, the presence of the inevitable telescreen reporting endlessly about the fact that the fleet would be back to E.F.I.S-1 in five months.

Deprived of love-dust, Imogen again ached for Eddie, longed for a personal message, however sanitised. She began to dream of her log cabin home back on Earth.

Abigail called in to see her once a day, chatting amicably about minor issues, never once referring to Imogen's detention or why it had happened.

Imogen tried to draw her out on the subject from time to time by asking, 'How long am I to be kept here?'

'As long as it takes.' Abigail's responses would be off-hand. 'Enjoy the lack of responsibility.'

'Am I to be punished for being in possession of love-dust?'

'Considering it's a capital offence, if that were, indeed, your crime, you would have been tried and convicted by now. We know Eddie gave you the love-dust. Equally, we know you wouldn't betray your own husband.'

'Will Eddie be in trouble on his return?'

Abigail would not be drawn on that one.

'Have there been any messages from him?'

Abigail hesitated.

'Have there? I can see from your face that the answer is "yes". Can't I have them relayed through to this room? What harm will it cause?'

'I'll see what I can do.'

Uncharacteristically, Imogen wanted to hold her, to kiss her, such was her gratitude for this faint promise.

'Can you get me some more love-dust?'

Abigail gave Imogen one of her hooded looks and left.

The interrogation was short, but not sweet. Imogen was faced by three senior Security people, their faces in the shade, whilst an unbearably bright light beat down on her. When one of her interrogators spoke in the darkness behind the light, she had no idea which one it was.

- Who supplied you with the beta-PXC9?
- My partner.
- His name?
- Edward Franks.
- How do you feel about him now?
- In what way?

- Do you love him?
- Yes, yes, I'm sure I do.
- You have no feelings of animosity towards him?
- No!
- When did you last use beta-PXC9?
- I can't remember. The day I was brought here. I don't know how long ago that was. I've lost all track of time.
- Do you crave beta-PXC9?

Hesitation, then:

- Yes. Yes. Please let me have some. Eddie. I need Eddie.

But they didn't let her have any. Not just then.

- Do you feel any hatred towards anybody?
- No.
- Abigail? Do you feel hated towards her?
- No. I don't think so.
- Are you sure?
- Yes, I'm sure.
- Do you feel any hatred towards us?
- No.
- We have something we wish you to watch. Please turn towards the screen.

A screen to her left flickered into life and filled with the images of small live mammals. They had been bred on E.F.I.S-1. Imogen was vaguely aware that such animals were used for laboratory experiments, but she didn't know how or why. They were nuzzling each other; some were mating.

- How do you feel towards such creatures?
- I don't really feel anything. One way or the other. I've never thought about them.
- These mammals have been injected with beta-PXC9. Continue to watch the screen please.

As Imogen watched, the creatures, normally benign, turned on each other. They bared vestigial fangs and fought. Those that were mating inflicted grave injury on their mates. It was a scene of terrible carnage. Imogen cried.

- What is your reaction to what you have just seen?
- It was horrible!
- Why did you find it horrible?

Imogen was unable to answer. How could anybody not find it horrible? The image faded and Eddie's face filled the screen. Her horror gave way to longing.

When she was returned to her quarters, a pot of love-dust was waiting for her by the recliner.

They allowed her to ingest beta-PXC9 once a day for a month. Then they returned her to the interrogation chamber and left her there. There were no interrogators present. She sat. The seats were empty.

Kreisler was on the telescreen. '*The problem we are encountering with beta-PXC9 is isomerisation. In layman's terms, this means that the molecular structure of the substance is changing. We call this isomer alpha-PXC9. It is no longer able to act against "aggression-chemicals". It gets worse. The shape of the molecule is now allowing it to block the actions of the "affection-chemicals". So the "aggression-chemicals" dominate, thus producing behaviour directly opposed to what we hoped would be the result.*'

They showed her the mammals devouring each other. She laughed. They showed her Eddie's face. She wanted to tear it to pieces.

Isomerisation.

As "Casa Nova" and the fleet returned home at the end of its peace mission, thermonuclear war was raging between Gallipoli and Ypres. Verdun had released a multi-megaton strike force against the mineral planets of E.F.I.S-1.

Crudely drawn pictures of flowers adorned the warheads.

THOMAS WADSWORTH is a short story author of speculative and dystopian fiction, as well as being a travel agent for charities.

"Third Closest to the Sun" is Thomas' first published story; he is currently shortlisted in the HG Wells Short Story Competition for his story, "The Second Door".

Thomas lives in Melbourne, Australia, with his wife and newborn son.

THIRD CLOSEST TO THE SUN

Daniel crawls through a mixture of mud and clothes. The pungent smell of jet fuel and acrid smoke fills and burns his nostrils. There is something else in the air, something he tastes as he breathes; a human smell. He spits, then composes himself before he continues to crawl past open suitcases and broken, twisted pieces of metal.

He hears the sound of a gas issuing from somewhere, the crackle of a fire, then a woman's moan. *Where?* He looks over his shoulder at the fuselage. He hears another moan. He stands and doubles over, hands on knees: a head rush. He stands again, turns, and staggers back to the wreck.

The metal cylinder is thirty metres long, with a gaping hole in the centre. Daniel walks in the shadow of the wing, which sticks up into the air at forty-five degrees. He peers inside. On the floor, which is now the ceiling, are rows and rows of seats. Most of the seats hold passengers who dangle from their waists, held in place with their safety belts. Some have their eyes open, some are closed. The new floor is littered with carry-on luggage freed from the lockers. Bodies lie in a heap; their arms and legs bent in contortions.

Daniel hears rapid breathing: in and out, in and out. His eyes dart about the cabin and locate movement. Fingers on a handball and flex.

'Hello?' he calls out.

No answer.

'Hello?' he calls again.

'Go. Away,' comes a reply, between gasps.

He steps into the plane, which creaks and sways with his weight. He edges forward and pauses beside a body. The glassy eyes point at the ceiling. He takes a breath and strides over the corpse. A few more steps and he sees the woman. Her face strained with focus. One hand holds her stomach, which is wet with blood. He reaches out.

'No. Leave me.'

Daniel retracts his hand, confused. 'I can help you.'

'No. Leave me.' Her breath is weak. 'Go. Away.'

Please let me help you.'

'I...said...no. I want. To die. I...have...never...died...like...this...before.'

Daniel stands outside the Soul Centre. The building is cold and sterile, with its white-washed walls and straight lines. The organisation's circular logo over the door, the only break from the perpendicular. The circle is split into two sections by a horizontal line, topped with a shining sun. The bottom section depicts various animals clambering on top of one another, forming a pyramid, frantically trying to reach the section above; a pyramid of desperate, frenzied humans reaching out of the circle towards the sun, towards the divine.

The wind whips through his hair. He puts his head down and proceeds towards the entrance. The door slides open. His eyes are drawn upwards to the glass roof, to the clouds and the heavens beyond. At ground level, people in suits and long white coats walk from room to room across the foyer. Daniel walks to the reception desk.

The receptionist, a young man, smiles at him. 'Can I help you?' His fingers hover over the keyboard in anticipation of Daniel's answer.

'No need, Jason.'

A woman in a lab coat, spectacles, and a name badge extends her hand. 'Great to see you again, Daniel. I'm Dr. Willmot. Come with me.'

He follows her around the reception to a lift in the rear wall. The doors open, and they step in. She faces Daniel and smiles. Her teeth are whiter than white.

'I can't wait to tell you the good news. It's exciting.'

He nods, puts his hands in his jean's pockets, and they watch the numbers on the lift light up.

'You are a totally different person to the man who walked into our building a month ago. Wouldn't you say?'

'I suppose.'

'You were confused and showed classic signs of depression. Now look at you.'

The doors open on the one-hundred and first floor. Daniel follows her down a corridor and through a pair of glass sliding doors into an open plan laboratory. More men and women mill about among tables, microscopes and computers. White coats, white tables, white walls.

The sliding doors close behind Daniel. Everyone in the room looks at him. His cheeks flush.

'It's him,' one of the doctors calls out.

Daniel is surrounded by smiling faces complimenting him.

'We're so happy to meet you, Daniel.'

'Yes, exciting times, Daniel, exciting times.'

He looks open-mouthed towards Dr. Willmot, who shoos the other doctors away and pulls him into her white office. She closes the door and offers him a seat.

'What was that about?' He sits down, squinting until his eyes adjust to the brightness.

Dr. Willmot pours a glass of water from a dispenser behind her gloss-white desk. She hands it to Daniel. 'Ice?'

'No thanks.'

She perches on the corner of her desk and places both hands in her lap. 'Daniel, you have paid us to provide you with a service and - the final payment has been received, right?'

'Yes, I think so.'

'Good, good. Well, you've paid us to provide you with a service and, boy, are you going to be satisfied with what you receive.'

He raises his eyebrows.

'You paid us for the premium service which is what you received. We are happy you did, as the findings were sensational. Over the past four weeks, we have been running tests; now, let me tell you the results.' She picks up a tablet from the table. 'I am so excited. Are you excited?'

'I guess so.'

'You will be. Your soul is almost evolved.' She straightens up, holds a hand to her chest and takes a breath.

'Almost? '

'Yes. Almost. It is one of the most evolved souls we have ever seen here at the Soul Centre.'

'What, um, does that mean? I was told some stuff in the previous visits, but there's a lot to take in.'

'Don't worry. I will explain the results. Right.' She flicks her finger over her tablet. 'At one point in time, we thought only the physical elements of a species evolved. For example, like how the eye came to be. We also believed that once an organism died, its soul left this world. At the Soul Centre, using a sophisticated process called soul mapping to pinpoint changes in a soul's energies, we know the soul evolves as well, and it does so through a process you will have heard of - reincarnation.' She taps the surface of the tablet, then continues: 'A soul travels through the lower life forms, like the grub and the worm, higher and higher, through cat, horse, lion, etc., peaking at the human form, the top of the cycle. Here is the important part, Daniel.'

He squints in concentration.

'Every time the human body dies, the soul "learns" from that route to death. Just like the gazelle which evolves to run faster and faster to escape its predator. Once the soul moves through the cycle and returns to human form, it's energies have changed, and it is "stronger" and "harder"; we have discovered that the body encasing it cannot suffer the same route to the base of the cycle 'again.'

'It can't die the same way?'

Dr. Willmot smiles, her eyes narrow as she does so. 'Correct. The more times the soul moves through the cycle, the more deaths its human body suffers, the more evolved the soul becomes. Soul evolution has nothing to do with Karma. It has everything to do with the expiration of the body encasing it. This explains why you survived the crash: your soul suffered a major impact in a former human

180

body which recommenced the cycle. It also explains why people are naturally immune to diseases.' She holds up a finger, and Daniel moves forward. 'The soul will evolve until it cannot die any more. When it reaches that point, it has reached divinity, and the human body will be as eternal as the soul it carries.'

He sits up. Eyes wide with hope. 'Are you saying I am immortal?'

'No.'

'Oh.' Daniel's shoulders sag. His fingers fidget.

'Do not dismay. You are carrying the most evolved soul we have encountered. It is great news.'

'So I'm not divine?'

'No, but once you die and your soul returns to human form, that body will be divine.'

'But not me?'

'It could be you. For instance, you could have been alive hundreds of years ago, but you can't remember, can you?' Dr. Willmot puts the tablet down and leans towards Daniel. 'Look, you shouldn't be disappointed. You are leading the human race to the next step of evolution. It's a one way ticket out of the constant animal-human cycle. Did you see our logo outside? You are on top of the pyramid; your hand is one of the closest to the sun.'

'One of?'

'You are third closest. There are two elderly ladies who are, by dint of their age, closer to divinity than you. They, too, have one more death to experience.'

'Only one more?'

'One more.' She holds up an erect finger.

He scratches his head and fluffs his fringe. 'Will I be like an angel?'

Dr. Willmot picks up a polished stone paperweight from her desk. 'Take the mineral. It has no concept of what it is to be a plant.' She points at the yucca in the corner of the room. 'Likewise, the plant has no concept of what it is like to be an animal. The animal has no notion of what it is to be human, to be able to understand that the world is round and that everything is made up of atoms. They have no idea. They cannot comprehend anything of the sort.' She puts the paperweight back on the desk. 'It's the same with the jump from the human form,' she touches her chest, 'to divinity.' She smiles at Daniel. 'We won't be able to guess at what it is to be angelic, as it will be more than you can ever imagine.'

Daniel's mouth opens in amazement.

'The universe will open up to a soul of that calibre,' says Dr. Wilmot, 'and the world will want to know you.'

Daniel jumps up from his seat. 'OK, I'm on for it. What do I have to do?'

Dr. Willmot reaches over her desk and opens a drawer. She pulls out a small, black apothecary bottle, with a pipette stopper. 'You live your life, Daniel.'

'But... how do I kill myself?'

She slides off the desk holding the palms of her hands towards him. 'Now, now. We don't condone suicide here.'

'Does that mean you're not going to tell me how to die?'

'We'll tell you, Daniel. Don't worry. We've studied your soul carefully; you paid for the premium service, you get the method *and* the means. As the Soul Centre is government funded, we need to insist that you lead a long and healthy life, before you make any quick decisions.'

'Why wait though, if divinity is so close? I could be the first.'

'You can do what you want, Daniel. I have to advise you what the government recommends.' She hands the small bottle to Daniel.

'What is this? '

'The means,' she replies.

Daniel opens the back door and stumbles into his kitchen. He smells fried mushrooms. He finds it offensive but, today, he doesn't care. There are unwashed dishes in the sink, muddy shoes left by the door. The cat's litter tray needs emptying. He feels irate at the sight of unfinished chores, but today he doesn't care.

'Hey honey,' Sandra says. She turns and spots the half-empty bottle in his hand. Her smile fades. 'What are you doing? '

'Drinking bourbon. The best bottle they had in store.'

She marches around the table. 'I mean, why are you drinking? Don't tell me you've been fired. Have you been fired? Don't say it, Dan. We need the money more than ever this month. There are so many bills.'

Daniel places the bottle on the cheap pine table and pulls up a chair. His lips twitch. He flicks the bottle cap, which skips off the table on to the floor. Sandra turns the stove off, then sits across the table from him. Daniel nods and touches his wife's hand. Her jaw tightens, but she places her hand on top of his.

'Tell me. What happened today?'

He looks into her tired eyes and says: 'You'll not understand, but I'll tell you anyway because you're my wife, so listen, as I'll only say this once.'

'Daniel?'

'I have,' he takes a breath, 'one of *the* most evolved souls anyone has ever encountered.'

Her hand slips from his. 'Sorry, what?'

'My soul will be the first to reach divinity. '

She pushes back her chair, and stands with her mouth agape.

He sits back and takes a swig from the bottle.

She places a hand on her forehead. 'You know how much they charge? Please say you haven't paid them yet?' She looks in his eyes. 'We've got no money, Daniel! How are we supposed to buy food for the kids, or pay those bills? I thought we talked about this. I thought you stopped going?' Her hands rake through her hair and she turns her back on him. 'They are con artists! They're selling a bullshit religion.'

'The government doesn't think so.'

She slams her hands on the table. 'The government is fucking moronic. They've pulled funding from legitimate scientific endeavours because of the fucking Soul Centre. They love the fact they are killing two birds with one stone by funding "scientific" progress *and* "religion".'

'All other research is a waste of money once you know the truth and the purpose.'

'I can't believe you.' She paces up and down the kitchen. 'The Daniel I knew before the crash was on the same page as me. You are in a totally different book now.'

'I started reading the right text.' He takes another swig of the bourbon.

'You're killing me. I wish you'd never seen that woman in the plane. I wish she had died before you got to her, then you'd have never got mixed up with those frauds.'

Sandra's eyes well up. She places a hand on the benchtop and sniffs hard. 'I can't breathe, Dan. I need you to understand that whatever you believe right now, we *need* the money returned. Please, go back and ask for a refund.'

Daniel shakes his head and rises from his seat. He grips the bourbon bottle around the neck and walks out of the kitchen. Sandra watches him enter the bathroom and hears him click the lock.

She runs up to the door. 'Dan, please, we can't live without that money. Come out and talk to me.' Her face is centimetres from the door. 'Come on, Dan, speak to me.'

She knocks gently.

'Dan? Are you listening to me?' The tears break and run down her face to her mouth. She can taste the salt.

She knocks louder, feeling the pain of her knuckles on the dense wood.

'Dan? Please answer me, Dan. Please.'

She presses her ear to the cold wood and hears a cap being unscrewed. She turns and sees the bourbon bottle cap on the kitchen floor. Her eyes dilate. Her chest heaves.

'Dan.' She bangs harder on the door. 'Dan, what are you doing in there? Dan?!'

She kicks the door and hammers it with both fists. 'Daniel!'

Also available from AudioArcadia.com:

Mary, A Twentieth Century Life
Climbing the Mast
Ain't Life Great!
An Eclectic Mix, Volume One
An Eclectic Mix, Volume Two
An Eclectic Mix, Volume Three

Due to be published shortly:

Ethereal Voices

AudioArcadia.com hold continuing short story competitions. Winning stories are published in paperback and eBook formats, then offered for sale worldwide on Amazon, Lulu and other relevant retail websites. Full details at www.audioarcadia.com/competition

www.ingramcontent.com/pod-product-compliance
Lightning Source LLC
Chambersburg PA
CBHW061135200626
46817CB00016B/1644